Unlocking Fire
A Bluebeard Retelling
Liv Strom

PUBLISHING

SM Press

Tales of Bones and Roses Series

Chronological order

- Ansa & Alexei – Unlocking Fire: A Bluebeard Retelling Novella (2023)

- Vanya & Dimitri – Stealing Glass: A Cinderella Retelling #1 (2023)

- Vanya & Dimitri – Claiming Glass Glass: A Cinderella Retelling #2 (2024)

- Ansa & Alexei – Spinning Fire: A Rumpelstiltskin Retelling (2024)

- Mariska & Kazimir – A Little Red Riding Hood Retelling *(2025)*

- Lana & Nikolai – A Beauty and the Beast Retelling *(upcoming)*

FREE Short Stories

Ansa & Alexei – Returning Home (2023) **Download NOW** on https://dl.bookfunnel.com/sxn3u3uzf7

CONTENTS

"My dear, you must not enter, nor even put the key into the lock, for all the world. If you do not obey me in this one thing, you must expect the most dreadful punishments."

Bluebeard

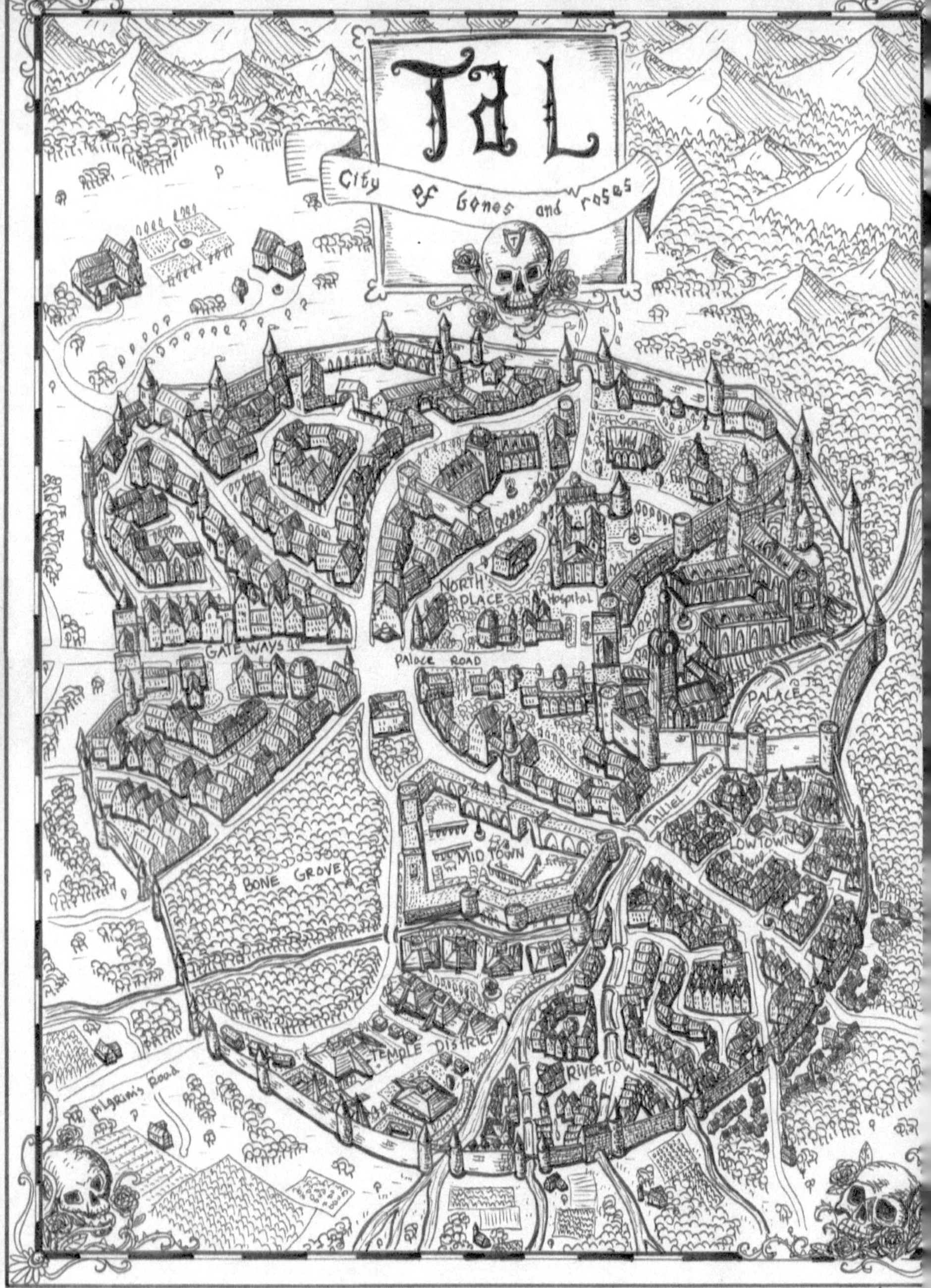

TAL
City of Bones and Roses
NORTH PLACE
Hospital
GATE WAYS
PAlACE ROAD
PALACE
TALLIEL - RIVER
LOW TOWN
BONE GROVE
MID TOWN
TEMPLE DISTRICT
RIVERTOW
Pilgrim's Road

Characters & Locations

Royals & Nobles

Dimitri Alexandre Ivanov – Crown Prince of Tal

Nikolai Alexandre Radanov – Prince of Tal

Mariska Yelena Radanova – Princess of Tal

Alexei Semyon Yurievich – Second son of a Talian country lord

Urs von Uster – Talian nobleman, head of the Roja, councilor

Rostya Ti Siniy – Talian nobleman

Commoners

Ansa – Server at the Drunken Dead drinking hall

Lanik – Owner of the Drunken Dead drinking hall

Popova – Lowtown apothecary owner, matchmaker, suspected
mage of unknown variety

Keep – Orchard worker

Path – Sorachian merchant

Neighborhoods of Tal

The Royal Palace

North's Place

Gateways

Bone Grove

Temple District

Midtown

Rivertown

Lowtown

Recorded Mages

Fire bearer – also known as known as explosions

Wind whisperer – also known as weather mages

Water seer – also known as seers

Earth mover – also known as growers

Sigil crafter – controlled by the Sigil Guild

Matter manipulator – also known as telekenetics

Hope holder – also known as healers

Heart turner – also known as mind witches

Death keeper – also known as necromancer

ANSA

I stepped inside Popova's shop, a gray, tense presence among the bright blues, warm maroons, and brilliant white of the other customers. They came from all over Tal for healing teas, fortifying concoctions, or—like me—favors.

Despite being located in Lowtown, Tal's poorest neighborhood, the shop was fine enough for well-to-do merchants and even some nobles. The tantalizing scents from the next-door bakery mixed with herbs and balms, rolling my sensitive stomach. I could afford none of it—belonged among the poor on the mud streets outside—but none of that mattered, because I was in dire need of a husband.

Before work the past three-day, I hovered next to the polished counter, requesting a meeting. And each day, the pretty women behind it, Popova's granddaughters and daughters-in-law, sent me on my way, for with one look, they knew I had nothing to trade. Until yesterday, when I finally convinced the youngest I had a secret valuable enough for Popova to meet with me and, hopefully, match me with one of her wealthy customers.

Popova—old, with Sorachian-dark skin despite her Vsadnik name, white-haired, and unbent—nodded to me from behind the counter.

This was it.

I had hoped for this moment for months, but now that it was here, desperation clawed at my insides. I knew I had no choice but to agree to anything she offered, for I would be without work and home by spring.

With one steadying breath, I straightened my spine and skirt, then followed her to the back door. Striding through the shop, more than one male eye lingered, making my skin too tight, breath too shallow. Even in Tal, where all ethnicities mixed as pilgrims arrived from mountains and coasts, I stood out. My red-blond hair, currently hidden as much as possible in a perfect bun, freckled skin, and height close to that of many men, drew attention no matter what I did. I looked like someone straight off the ships from Mjors. *Blend*, Grandpa had lectured me, *give no one a reason to look under the surface*. Impossible, when you stood out like a pale candle.

A gentleman in a fur-lined red coat smirked at me. If I paused he might look at my hair and tell me he needed something to match it. Or reach for my overheated skin. I hurried my steps. Beauty had gotten me into this. This was its chance to get me out.

In the back room, Popova had already poured us tea and settled on the velvet seating cushions. Lowtown might be the poorest neighborhood in Tal, but no one would dare to rob Popova. Not only did she have nine strong sons guarding her properties, everyone knew she was a mage. People disagreed what kind—sigil crafter, water seer, wind whisperer, or even a death keeper or heart turner. Each tale changed her abilities. Those in the store queued for her concoctions—be it to fall in love, regrow hair, or improve health. Only high nobles were accepted by the healers at the hospital. The rest of us had Popova. For my purpose, none of it mattered. I only needed Popova, the woman, who could acquire anything for a price.

"What's your name, girl?" she asked, looking me up and down.

"Ansa. Thank you for seeing me." I lifted the teacup, suppressing the tremors in my hand.

"My favorite granddaughter insisted you know something valuable enough to make this worth my while. You keep coming, asking for a husband. Why?"

"It's time." I stopped my hand from drifting to my belly, but she must have caught the twitch.

"Ah, and how much time?"

"Three months." I tensed my fingers around the cup. "I'm keeping it."

She nodded. "Life's life. But my clientele is distinguished. Why don't you marry a nice stable boy? With your looks, I'm sure you could twist his head quick enough."

I sipped the fresh mint tea to calm my mind and suppress the fire churning in my belly. "I don't want a stable boy. I want the child to have more than I did. A real education. Become a noble." In Tal, only they were safe, especially with the blood this child carried. "Please under—"

She raised her wrinkled hand. "I know the complaints of the desperate and dreamers. If that's what you ask, you're both. No rich stranger will take you in for nothing, solving all your problems. Leave and—"

"Not until you listen."

Popova frowned at my interruption. "Tell me who got you into this position, and I'll make sure he regrets it. Might even do it for free. But when your belly swells directly after the wedding, any man with sense would know he was scammed. You might think me powerful. They do not. I'll not risk my reputation for you."

I listened, knowing every word was true, then raised my hand.

There was only one argument I could give. One thing that might overcome my lack of breeding—*Magic*. Something that made my child an asset instead of a burden.

I relaxed my control a fraction, and the air above my hand caught fire. The flickering flame burned from yellow to red to hottest blue before I closed my fingers and absorbed it back into my heated blood. It was the most magic I dared. Letting it out loosened other inhibitions. Most mages were not dissimilar to drunks: seduced by the aftereffects of the mind-altered state and doomed to end in the gutter or dead long before adulthood. Grandpa had not even lit a candle with his power. If I ever lost control of the blaze inside, I was likely to burn everything around me before mage's illness killed me. Even nobles trained from birth were known to fall—only then did you learn of their power. In life, they kept it hidden. All knew never to anger a noble for you did not know what they might be capable of.

As my brief light disappeared, Popova's eyes glittered.

"Fire bearer." She smiled, showcasing gilded teeth. "What family?"

"They've got nothing to do with this. It comes from my grandfather. I'm the only one who inherited the power."

"Most are consumed by it before they're grown."

I nodded jerkily. I rarely let the fire out, because one day, I would not be able to extinguish it again. Fire bearers had another name—explosions.

"And the father?" Popova nodded pointedly at my belly, avarice glittering in her eyes.

"He's the same." That was what drew me to Path, why I had believed his promise to marry and take me away after meeting at the night market. He powered the Sorachian steam machines with his fire without shame. His every movement, the support from his family who did not flinch away, had promised a freedom I had not even dared to dream of. In Tal, not even nobles used their powers like that. Magic was secret, revered and dangerous. Never casual or practical.

I shared Path's bed from that night, listening to tales from the coast. For the first time, did not fear the heat under my skin when close to another. Then two nights before summer ended, I woke up alone, Path's caravan already far from Tal.

Popova poured me another cup of tea, her demeanor transforming from dismissive to calculating. "I have a customer—he has come here for years—who has been searching for the perfect wife. Lord Siniy is double your age, richer than all of Lowtown put together and, if he approves of you, has a history of short engagements."

"He'll marry me?"

Popova's eyes twinkled. "When he sees you, he'll owe me."

My bunched shoulders should have eased; gratitude should have flooded my eyes. A better person would have kissed Popova's hands in thanks. I only stared at my own, at a wrinkle in my starched skirt, breaking the controlled perfection. My involuntarily clenching hands had done that, showcasing an emotion I could not allow to escape. I tugged at the worn, striped fabric, making it worse before stroking it flat with too-hot hands.

When it was smooth, I finally raised my eyes, outwardly calm. "And my child?"

"I'll inform the lord. No deceiving such a man." Her perceptive eyes dug into mine. "Are you ready to be owned by another?"

"Yes," I said, biting down on the "nos" and "not yets." Grandpa taught me to be pragmatic. *Take what life gives you, make out of it what you can, and look no further.* It was not likely he had expected to raise a five-year-old girl alone. Expectations killed you. Like my mother, who had expected a normal child.

I signed away my life, promising to follow Popova's instructions, and escaped while smothering the fire that sought a way out. I knew there was none. I had a power that would never make me anything beyond a weapon or a breeding mare. That was what Grandpa told me when he made me promise never to tell anyone. If I had not broken my word, showed Path the fire that always threatened to escape through my cracks, I would not have been in this situation.

Popova promised to inform me when the meeting with my future husband was arranged. All I could do until then was get back to serving in the drink hall, earning what coins I could, for when the pregnancy showed, Lanik would surely let me go and Odilia's—the boarding house for single women on 15 Ulna Street I had called home the last two years—would kick me out.

Outside Popova's neat shop, the world split into a new before and after, as it had when I found out I was with child. Like my life was a series of choices breaking me apart. Would I end up all jagged pieces? And, when I had peace and quiet, could I fit them together again?

I should have been relieved—I had achieved what I set out to do—but the fire inside did not want to settle, and, despite my normally impeccable control, it took all my focus to keep it locked up.

Marriage is better than becoming a weapon, I told myself, knowing all Popova's services had a price. What would mine be?

The question spun through my mind as I started my shift at the Drunken Dead, serving drinks and stew I did not want to look too close at. If Lord Siniy did not want me, could I convince Lanik, owner and barkeep, to let me stay even when I showed? He had pinched my backside enough times for me to guess what he would ask in return. But even that would only delay the problem. I could never leave this child in the care of another. Not if they burned like I had.

As the sun set, I missed orders and bumped into tables, the fire rolling inside. I needed to regain control. I needed to know if Lord Siniy was as dangerous as the nobles Grandpa told of, or if he was the savior I had prayed to the Wishmaker for.

CHAPTER TWO

ALEXEI

Somehow, the glass was empty. Again. And so was the bottle. Neither had held any answers, so without looking up, I waved to refill it, hoping they would come with another helping. Normally I would not indulge like this, but after yesterday, nothing was normal.

I had failed Dimitri—the as of last night exiled Crown Prince of Tal, my best friend, and childhood partner in mayhem. As second son to a country lord, I might seem set to the people drinking in this run-down hall on the edge of Rivertown, but in the palace, I was barely above a peasant. Not that I wanted to get involved in the race to the top. With Dimi, there had been no need. All he had expected in return for his favor was that I stand by his side, and Wishmaker, had I been useless. The sigil ring on my finger glittered as if reminding me I still had something to lose. The Roja, the infamous royal spies and assassins, might come at any moment to snatch me up—though by avoiding my usual hangouts, I hoped to delay the inevitable.

When the next drink failed to arrive, I searched the rowdy room and spotted hair like flame. It should have been flowing free; instead, a strict bun tried to hide it, like the starched gray-and-white-striped dress tried to hide the woman. An impossibility.

With a tray of glasses held above her head, she swung around patrons, delivering and taking orders without pause. The practiced, efficient movements seemed to happen without conscious thought because her eyes were far away, and concern wrinkled her forehead. I tried to catch her attention for more than a drink. A distraction, even if it was only an exchange of words, was just what I needed—and she could distract anyone.

She picked up another round from the bar, ignoring me. As she passed, I snatched a bottle meant for another off the tray and placed coins, including a good tip, in its place—hopefully enough to earn me a smile. She twisted, ready to take the wine back, when a giant man, further into his cups than me, rose behind her.

It seemed the woman would notice and move out of the way, but she was still focused on the bottle in my hand, blinking with ice-blue eyes, like she had just woken up. She reached for the coins next to the remaining bottles and cups on her tray as the mountain of a man at her back staggered. I tried to pull her out of the way. She jumped back from my raised hand.

"Don't you—"

I opened my mouth to warn her.

Too late.

They collided. Glass splintered into a million shards, wine flowed, and patrons cursed. I vaulted over my table and caught the redhead before she hit the floor. I'm not sure I'd ever had a more satisfactory use of the fine reflexes drilled into me since arriving in at the palace.

"Watch what you're doing!" the man bellowed, catching his balance.

"What *I'm* doing?" I set the woman down behind me.

The intoxicated giant stood as tall as me, which few do, strong from manual labor I had never experienced, and in search of an enemy. His eyes narrowed on my fine coat, silver buttons, and empty belt. Maybe I should start carrying a weapon to better save damsels in distress. Or think before I act.

A scorching hand closed around my wrist. Before I could question it, the heat lowered to a simmer, and I swallowed the numerous curses fighting to get out. No way I wanted the man before me to think I was insulting *him*.

He stumbled forward until only a handspan separated us. Wishmaker, he was a big guy. As he grunted, the hand on my wrist burned, and I could not hold in the curse on my tongue. "*Mother-Goddess-Bastard*!"

The giant's face twisted in rage as he howled, "Don't take the Goddess's name in vain!"

Before the last word was out, he swung.

I tried to duck, I really did, but despite my well-executed heroic dash and the centering pain in my wrist, I was still equal parts wine and sense.

With a smack, he grazed my jaw. In defense, I spun as taught and, using his momentum, my elbow connected perfectly with his temple. He dropped like an ox. My trainers would have been proud. Or possibly satisfied. Growing up with the crown prince had been a constant parade of the best tutors in everything. Sometimes, I had even listened before sneaking toads into their armor.

I turned with a satisfied grin. Seemed a brawl had been just what I needed to knock me out of my thoughts. Hopefully, the fire-headed beauty would be thankful.

Instead of grateful eyes and a warm embrace, I found her with her back to mine and arms raised in pacification. It seemed the ox had friends with arms the size of tree trunks. *A lot* of friends.

They moved to surround us, cracking knuckles.

"Shouldn't have done that," giant number two said, his dark, weather-worn skin seeming to deepen his already impressive frown. "Should've taken it and left."

"It's a misunderstanding. Please," the woman said as I pulled her to my side. No way I would hide behind her.

The circle around us tightened, the glass crunching under heavy boots. "Only thing missing 're our drinks."

"I cannot cover them. Your friend stepped into me," she said, sounding resigned despite her words. "You all saw it."

Guilt sloshed inside me. It had been my fault. Her desperate tone merged with my little sister's when she begged me to stay, knowing each farewell was inevitable. This woman did not expect any favors from the world. But there was always a way out.

I looked between the smashed glasses and the man slowly regaining consciousness. Maybe one bothered them more than the other.

"Be ready to run," I said to the server, then threw one of my last two purses to the barkeep, who, like every other patron, watched our standstill. My future was in turmoil, finances hanging on by a thread, but I still had more than most here would ever know. I raised my voice, saying, "A drink for all this fellow's friends on me."

The belligerent men barely beat the other guests to the bar. Seemed everyone knew a fellow when the tap was open. I grabbed the woman's hand and pulled her outside before the money ran out. Luckily, she came without argument, realizing they might well turn our way again as soon as their glasses were filled.

The busy night greeted us, despite the winter winds smelling of first snow blowing down from the mountains. Tal, the City of Bones and Roses, came alive when the sun set and the Spirits of the dead rose. No one knew why or where they went during the daylight hours, but at night, the world's dead gathered in our ancient city, and so did the mourners. The glowing, diffuse white shapes, which could be neither distinguished between nor communicated with, despite what some might claim, were thickest in the Temple District and Bone Grove, but outside the palace's sigil-covered walls, there was not a street in Tal left completely dark at night.

Masses of pilgrims, rich and poor, filled the city during summer to pay their respects to their ancestors and trade. They had slowed to a trickle now that winter had settled—only those determined to make Tal their home remaining—but the Talians kept their nocturnal ways and roused themselves with the Spirits. Only the palace was different, and I visited the city rarely enough that the children playing tag in the semidarkness seemed strange.

We slowed after crossing the first bridge and entering Rivertown proper, where cobbled streets replaced frozen mud, regular lanterns colored the night, and criers stood in every doorway advertising food or paid company. The arms of the Taliell divided the houses, barges closed for winter lined the canals, and a hundred bridges arched over the dark water.

When we crossed the ancient Dragon Bridge, the redhead narrowed her eyes and tore her hand from mine. I instantly missed its warmth.

"I could've handled it," she snapped. "How much did you even throw at them? I cannot repay you."

"I wasn't expecting you to." It had, after all, been my fault. A thoughtless way to catch her attention.

"Maybe in a few months," she continued, as if she had not heard me. "If all goes well. Or sooner. Tell me how much and—"

To halt her tirade, I placed a hand on her shoulder, warm despite her thin dress, and gave her my best smile. The worse I felt, the wider it stretched. It had for years been my penultimate defense when caught doing something I should not—when even that failed, I'd run the other way while pushing Dimi's younger cousin at anyone who caught us somewhere we were not supposed to be. No one could resist little Mariska's big eyes or would punish the youngest member of the royal family. My smile wavered. She was another reason to leave the life I had built.

Shaking my head, I sighed.

"Don't give me that look. Everyone wants payment," the woman said with narrowed eyes.

"The look wasn't for you. Well, the smile was."

"Keep that as well. I have no use for it."

Her eyes glittered and wisps of hair escaped the bun, dancing in the wind. She looked at my hand, still resting on her shoulder, and paled in fright.

I reluctantly stepped back—far be it for me to push myself on someone unwilling. My mother had taught me better, and the thought of anyone taking advantage of my sister was one of the few things that would make me want to return to Sizov, my family home outside Denyev.

The woman still stared at my hand. I followed her gaze.

My green coat sleeve hung in charred tatters. I pulled it away, revealing blisters covering part of the swirling noble's sigil encircling my forearm. It was placed on me at birth, showing my House and forcing me to obey its Head, currently my uncle, thankfully far away. The golden ring on my finger caught the light, as if to confirm my ancestry.

My wrist bore an angry red shape of a small hand, with two painful blisters where thumb would have met forefinger. I brushed over them. Definitely painful, definitely new, but not serious.

"You're noble. I never meant to..."

The woman looked ready to bolt, her eyes searching for escape. Hurting a noble in Tal led at best to a stay at our infamous prison. Hidden magic, supposedly reserved for the nobility and a dangerous liability to anyone else, could lead to a different kind of cage.

My lips twitched. "Seems you were right. You didn't need my help after all."

"I'm not a..."

"Mage," I offered when it seemed she could not even say the word.

She retreated until her back pressed against the bridge's stone pillars and its lanterns painted her in shadows and light. A Spirit drifted across the water, illuminating us from below.

I raised my hands to show I meant no harm.

"Wait before going back. They might still take issue as the money will have run out by now." I tried the smile again. "I'm barely even a noble. Just a second son, probably illegitimate."

I waited, knowing I could have just left but did not want to.

Her eyes drifted to my exposed sigil again before meeting my gaze and straightening her skirts, composed, as if all that had happened was tucked away far inside, like the wonderful hair she repined until not a strand escaped.

"You won't report me to the Roja."

It was not a question. Still, I shook my head. "And you won't burn me to cinders."

Her smile—small, restrained, despite herself—lit up my night brighter than any lantern could have. How did this woman think she could hide?

"I'm not normally that easily spooked," she said.

"Didn't seem spooked. I'm the one who threw away my money and ran. I'm Alexei, by the way."

"Don't you have a long, complicated title?"

"Don't you have a name? It's polite to exchange one for the other."

She sized me up, like her name was a weapon she did not share lightly.

"Ansa." She stared at my sigil and singed skin again before shaking her head. "I have to head back, or Lanik won't pay me... All those bottles... What if he broke the chair? I can't afford to lose this job."

"I'm sorry. Let me walk you. If anything more was destroyed, I'll pay," I said, knowing I would have to start selling my possessions soon. Still, she hesitated. I should have let it go; she had every right to walk away, and I had only given her trouble, but my mouth kept going. "It's for my own benefit, really. Without you, I would still be brooding."

I extended my arm. Instead of accepting, she pointed to the right.

"That way's closer."

I ruefully realized she was not a lady expecting to be led around. Considering her magic, she might even prefer to not touch at all. So when we walked, I ensured the sliver of air between us remained even when the house walls on both sides pressed in.

Ansa directed me through the warren of alleys separating leaning apartment buildings hung with laundry. Here, true dark hid our features, and without distractions, her unnatural warmth stood out every time we almost brushed against each other.

"Why were you brooding?" she asked, breaking the silence before it grew uncomfortable.

"A friend of mine suffered a misfortune and his father sent him out of Tal." Even saying that much bordered on treason. But talking had always helped me process and she was a stranger far away from the court. The downside of being friends with the crown prince was that your experiences were not yours to share. Especially not these ones. "Without him, I might have to leave Tal."

"There must be more for you here than one friend."

I could not tell her he was the crown prince, or of the potential fallout of me supporting his actions. That while I could leave the death, poverty, and politics of Tal behind, my father would ask why I had not made something of myself yet—having inherited none of his magic and looks, I could not see him without questioning my parentage. I knew the feeling was mutual.

Neither could I say that as soon as my mother heard of Dimi's exile—and she would hear from one of her many correspondents—she would ask me to return home, insisting Tal and the king were too dangerous. I shared part of the blame for it going so far for I had known about the elopement of the Talian heir and kept silent.

And I could certainly not tell Ansa the Roja might be following me this very moment, ready to take me away. I had known it violated Dimi's engagement to a foreign princess he had never met, and still helped him arrange it. People had been executed for less.

Then there was the immediate concern of covering my living costs. With Dimi gone, the castle keeper would surely find me and demand payment.

All good reasons encouraging me to leave, except how could I then stand by Dimi's side when he returned and make up for freezing when they dragged him away?

My gut clenched. I looked over my shoulder, finding darkness that could conceal anything. Even the Spirits of the dead seemed to hide from the winter winds. Waiting for something to happen—for the Roja to find me—was almost as much torture as what was sure to come.

Realizing I had let the silence stretch too far, I offered Ansa the memories I could share. The happy times not too long ago.

"I love Tal. Love my time here. There were four of us, inseparable since we were children in the Women's Tower, causing mayhem and playing pranks. One's in love with my friend, and he in her. His father forbid the marriage and sent his son away. Naturally, the bride is taking what happened and my friend's absence even harder than me. As far as I know, she has not left the Tower since. The other is his little cousin. Unfortunately, it seems she imagined us all matched up."

"And you don't desire to be matched?"

"She's wonderful, pretty and I don't know anyone who would deserve her. Certainly not me."

From Ansa's scoff, she must have heard the grin in my voice.

"So, you're too busy with others to settle down with this nice woman, who is clearly from a good family. Just the kind I always seem to come across."

"Riska's like a little sister who now makes moony eyes at me. And what's wrong with not wanting a family? I plan to never marry and make no secret of it. And her House is part of what is too good for the likes of me."

"Not everyone can afford to reject a good family, no matter the reason," she said, the teasing tone gone. "Do you know Lord—"

Scraping feet interrupted her. I paused, listening. The sound, clearly footsteps, came from both behind and ahead. We were trapped. They had found me. Why had I thought the Roja less likely to grab me from the streets of Lowtown? Here, the only witness would be Ansa. If they let her leave.

I should have insisted on staying on the main roads. Should also have kept at least a knife on me.

"Thieves," she whispered as a lantern shutter clicked and low light chased the darkness away.

I pushed Ansa down and to the side, praying to the Wishmaker she was right. My only chance was to have space to move, and I was not putting her between me and my opponents again. Hopefully, they had not seen her and would assume me alone.

The light outlined a man too large to be a coincidence. As he spoke, the voice—soberer, harder, but unmistakable—confirmed it. It was the man from the drink hall I'd hit. My stomach unclenched. No Roja. Not yet.

"Thought we would find you sneaking back. See, the coin paid for the wine. We still owe you a beating."

They chuckled.

I waved for Ansa to scooch into a doorway. There was no point in knocking in this part of town, but the shadows would hide her better. I could take a beating well enough if needed. Dimi usually bashed me in the training yard daily.

"The money wasn't enough?"

"Figured a man who throws away a purse to protect a girl has another one on him," a man said from behind. We were trapped. "Barkeep said she would be back. Take a chance and the Wishmaker rewards you."

I placed my back to the doorway, keeping both the approaching men in my peripheral vision. Given a moment, I would have pulled out the other coin purse. Not that they would have trusted that was my only one without stripping me. I had severely miscalculated, or drink combined with beauty had robbed me of my usual sense. Whys no longer mattered.

They moved as one. I dodged the first fist, diverted the second, but there was no time to strike back or space to move before the third connected.

Desperately, I kicked the knee out of the right-side man on my way down. Focusing on my opponent cost me.

I hit the ground hard, knocking the air out of my lungs. Gasping for breath, seeing a foot stomp down, I knew it was over. Hopefully, when I blacked out, they would take the money and leave me with my life. Hopefully, they would not see Ansa. Another foot came. My ribs screamed in pain, my lungs for air.

Distracted yet? a voice inside mocked. I should not have mixed with my betters. Should not have tried to hide. Who was I to think I could escape the Goddess's judgment?

Ansa's eyes reflected the light.

Their shine increased, and I knew it was not from the hooded lantern. Fire burned inside her.

I clenched my eyes shut and pressed into the frozen mud as heat passed over me with a *swoosh*, accompanied by screams and retreating feet.

The flames did not stop. As if alive, they spiraled above us, scorching the air. I crawled forward through the now soft dirt and placed a hand on her ankle.

"They're gone. You'll torch all of Tal. *Ansa, stop.*"

Even through her leather boot, she was almost too hot to touch. Since before we settled in the cities, humans were primed to flinch away from fire, and most of me wanted nothing more than to flee with our attackers. But this woman had saved my skin despite me getting us into this situation.

Keeping my voice calm, I babbled, trying to reach her. "Do you want to hear a secret?" Her blue eyes shone, unseeing. "I shouldn't say anything, but you won't tell, right? Tal almost changed yesterday, though few know it." The flames hesitated, as if they desired to consume my words more than my flesh. "Your future king, my best friend, almost married for love at the temple. The current king forbade it. He was furious. Even scarier than you. I stood there and let them drag Dimi away, and now I cannot face myself. Don't burn me off this world before I have a chance to make it up to him."

The fire retreated until only afterimages shone before my tearing eyes.

"Thank you, Goddess, for taking none of us this night," I said, finally believing I would live at least another day.

Ansa did not move. Did not blink as light and heat still swirled around her raised hands. Her narrow shoulders shook, a whimper escaping her clenched teeth. Freckles previously barely visible stood out like burns on her too-pale skin.

I should have retreated and allowed her privacy. We did not know each other. She was a mage without control over her magic, lost in her own mind. But when my sister had one of her episodes, shaking uncontrollably and at risk of injuring herself, only one thing helped. So against my better judgement—which I had ignored the entire night anyway—I reached out, placing a hand on her too-hot wrist. When she did not flinch away, I wrapped her in my arms slow enough for her to pull away. She did not.

I ignored the heat and squeezed her, anchoring her to the now, mumbling nonsense about my life. I held her through the shock, taking at least as much comfort from her as she did from me, strangely comfortable sitting on the winter street. Her body temperature lowered from a furnace to comfortable, and as long as I did not move, I could ignore my various injuries.

Slowly, her too-wide, unnaturally shining blue eyes focused on me.

"I'm so sorry. Did I hurt you?" Her voice was laced with panic, body shaking. "I lost control."

"You saved me."

She pulled away and I let her, the awkwardness growing with the distance as we both remembered we were strangers. Without another word, we left the alley, pausing under a lantern to study each other. Despite the last bell, she was no less beautiful as she straightened her mud-stained dress. Her hands moved on to check each pin in her hair, and despite the ruined clothes, she had a bearing worthy of any lady.

"Is it true?" she asked when centered and as proper as possible given the circumstances, her eyes filled with emotions I could not decrypt.

"Which part?"

"That you know the crown prince?"

I nodded. No point in denying it now.

"If I asked you for information on another noble, would you tell me the truth?"

"I endangered you twice and now owe you my life." I looked away, guilt warming my cheeks. What if someone caused this much trouble for my sister because he could not wait for his drink? "I owe you all the answers you want, and even if I didn't, I would offer them. Bear in mind, I really am hardly a lord."

"Do you know Lord Siniy? Is he a good man?"

"Has he done you wrong?"

She hesitated before answering, tension hardening her body. "Not yet, but like your prince, I'm set to marry, and all I know of my groom is his name."

I ransacked my memories from years at court, parties, and state dinners, coming up empty. Seemed I had no more answers for Ansa than for myself. "I've never heard of him."

She blinked in surprise. "Is that unusual?"

"There are more than a hundred Houses in Tal, and as many on the countryside. But if he attended court..."

I would have at least recognized the name. Dimi never cared for gossip, but it was the one currency I usually had a lot of.

The silence stretched and Ansa's face pinched like she was swallowing her pride. "Could you find out? If I just knew he was good..."

Again I thought of my sister Zora, pleading to join me in Tal, knowing it could not be. I had asked the Wishmaker for a chance to be useful. For a distraction. I smiled and bowed in my singed coat.

"Your wish is my command."

Talians usually married on the last day of summer, but it seemed this winter would be full of ill-considered unions.

Chapter Three

Ansa

Since I returned two nights ago, smelling of smoke and looking like I rolled in the dirt, Lanik's beady eyes had followed me, and though I knew he could not, the voice inside screamed that *he knew*.

The last time I lost control was when my sister stole my only doll. In my anger, the flames burned them both, though the scorched wallpaper was the only thing to not survive. The shouts had summoned our mother, her face warped by shock and anger. The next thing I remember was the freezing water of the Taliell closing above me, my mother's hands pushing down as mine clawed at hers in confusion, fear, and mindless desperation.

She said I could—and given a chance, would—kill everyone. Grandpa's strong hands had pulled me out, shaking and heaving water. This time, Alexei—a stranger who should have condemned me and ran—held tight, pulling me back. Embarrassment coiled inside me, a spring pulling tighter and tighter under Lanik's shrewd stare.

As I prepared the hall for the evening crowds, embers traveled under my skin, flaring with my anger every time I passed him. There was a good chance he had encouraged the men to go after Alexei, thinking their absence would prevent a bar fight and that they would return to the Drunken Dead to spend their loot. I had seen it before. At least Alexei had not brought the City Guard to arrest us all.

Morning sickness and anxiety fought for my attention, as I hoped for Alexei and answers every time the door swung open. His embrace had been an invasion of privacy, too much too fast, and felt too safe.

The door slammed again, and my head snapped around. The pretty girl I'd badgered and cajoled to allow me to see Popova marched up to me. She ignored the early drunks and Lanik, handing me a note with a meaningful nod. I sounded each letter in my mind, stringing the syllables together though they seemed to wiggle away, until I could understand each word. *Meet Siniy at the apothecary in a bell. Do not arrive late.* I had already wasted a quarter.

Inventing an excuse for Lanik, promising to be back as soon as I could, I ran to my rented room, changed, then scrubbed my face, hands, and neck. It was the best I could do.

If this did not work, I would have to find a common man to trick, but how could anyone other than a noble hide a child cursed with fire? Grandpa had trained me to keep it all inside, but I held no confidence I could do the same for the life I carried. Most mages succumbed to madness. Had Alexei not been there to draw me back the other night, with his rambling truths and steady hands, I might have burned all of Rivertown.

In my best dress, with cheeks flushed and heart pounding, I passed the elaborate glass beakers in Popova's display window and entered the shop.

The girl, now behind the counter, ushered me into the private back room already prepared for my suitor's arrival. Scents of cinnamon, cloves, and butter lay heavy in the air, and I wished to rush upon the prepared table, having thrown up my last meal—this visit clearly warranted more than tea. Instead, I sat and checked my hair and dress, as if perfecting them could disguise how badly I would fit as a noble's wife. I remembered the sigil lines winding around Alexei's burned wrist like a shackle—would I get the same if I married Lord Siniy?

A hard knock sounded against the door. I could not help leaning forward as my breathing hitched and heart raced.

Looks and fire got you into this, I reminded myself and forced the corners of my lips up. *Perhaps a pretty smile will help solve it.*

Popova entered first, her frown seeming to say, *Don't dare to make me look bad,* before stepping aside to reveal my future husband, the man my child might call Father.

The first thing I thought when I saw Lord Siniy was that I would never have noticed him on the street. He was neither short nor tall, skin neither white nor black, of average build, and could be anywhere between forty and sixty. His neatly trimmed beard held more gray than the blue-black of his hair. He was a mix of all that was Talian, his ancestry possibly as eclectic as the city itself. Even his fine wool clothes were of excellent cut but discreet. The lord was not a man who wished to draw attention to himself. Only his dark eyes, hungry when they landed on me, spoke of anything outside the ordinary.

I shivered under his scrutiny, though I could not deny my own judgment. He was older than I desired, but I had known I was not his first wife. It could have been much worse, and his stately bearing was better than a more flamboyant husband. Control was everything for someone like me, and a calm life was a necessity rather than preference.

I stood as he bowed.

"You asked me long ago to call on you if I found someone who reminded me of your last wife. This is Ansa. I hope you find her suitable." Popova gave me a firm look and exited before I had time to even greet her.

No lady would have been left alone with a suitor. But I was neither lady nor pure.

"The likeness is remarkable," Siniy said, then held my hand as I sat.

Embers seemed to claw under my skin. It took all my focus to keep the fire in check. No one would be scorched again.

He settled opposite me.

"Is your past wife recently deceased?" I asked, hoping it was not too forward.

"Nearly eight years now. She died soon after the wedding." Siniy sipped his tea. "I hear you already carry a potential heir."

"I'm sorry, my lord." My cheeks warmed and palms sweated. "It doesn't have to be an heir."

He smiled as if to a child. "From what Popova tells me, it will be *just right*. But there can be no secrets between us. As my wife, you will have access to everything, manage the household and draw any funds you want. I only ask you to respect my word."

He let go of my hand and meticulously placed three gold coins bearing the crossed bones of Tal on the table, one on top of the other, then pushed them to the center. A clear offering if I dared to reach for it. More wealth than I had ever possessed. Had ever seen.

My hand, flat against my skirts, itched.

If I accepted, I would be safe from poverty. My child would be trained. If we became ill, a healer would be summoned to care for us. We would get respect, if not from the nobles, then at least from others. Now, I had nothing.

The gold glittered. My heart pounded in my ears. My hand twitched, then snatched up the coins, as if it acted on its own accord, and if fast enough, it would mean less.

With the heavy, cold wealth clenched between my fingers, I raised my eyes to Siniy's.

"You know best, my lord. I'm happy to be yours." His smile grew, the tension in the air shifted, and the fire inside me flared. I forced it down. "What kind of life should I expect?"

"I live simply. Few parties or guests, and my privacy is of uttermost importance." His eyes glittered as they drifted down to my covered chest. "My research is my passion."

"Research?"

"The origins of magic. Many believe the gods select certain people—nobles—and bless them. I will prove it sits in the blood, more precisely the heart."

He nodded, having never taken his eyes off my chest, or heart perhaps, as if he could pierce the layers of cloth, skin, and flesh.

I licked my lips before suppressing my unease. "How... noble."

He met my gaze again, and the hunger I had seen before had grown a hundredfold. I often saw similar emotions reflected in the eyes of men, thought they no longer bothered me. I had been wrong.

"I believe you have something to show me," he said.

For a moment, I thought he meant for me to undress. But his eyes had traveled to my hands. Lifting the one not gripping the coins, I swallowed my reluctance.

With Popova, it had felt liberating, like claiming my power. With Alexei, there had been acceptance. Under Siniy's dark eyes, the flame dancing over my hand was a surrender. It reduced me to a mystery to be solved, an item to be collected.

"*Wonderful.*"

A fire bearer was never cold, and still, a chill swept through me as I saw my light reflected in his eyes. Clenching my hand, I drew in the flames, despite their desperate desire to escape and burn and burn and burn, reminding me that between me and Siniy, I was the monster.

He smiled, flashing perfectly straight, white teeth. "Excellent. I'll make all the arrangements and summon you when ready. Settle your affairs, Ansa, because you will not return."

My salvation sounded like the hangman's steps. *It's only fear of change. The loss of control*, I told myself, while praying to the Wishmaker Alexei would return with tales to calm my nerves. In Tal, all knew love and death were unavoidable. Smiling at my future husband, I feared which one awaited me.

Siniy reached for the treats prepared for his visit with sudden vigor. The cloying scents, the flaking dough and spices I had longed for, rolled my stomach as I watched him eat.

My child would be born noble and be afforded the best tutors.

I would have the finest dresses and food.

Nothing untoward had been said or done.

Love can come with time, I told myself as a tear evaporated on my cheek. A fire bearer cannot afford to be ruled by emotions.

Breathing deeply, I shut each one down like Grandpa had taught me and longed for his guidance as I sat through the first meal with my future husband. Siniy had done nothing wrong, been a perfect gentleman, and I had taken his coin. It was done. Still, I needed to know he was a good man more than ever.

I pressed my hand against my still-flat belly under the table and imagined I could feel the child growing inside. The embers moved through my blood, crawled under my skin, and I knew that if I found no control over my new life, the wedding might be too late. All I could hope for was a drunk country noble's promise to find answers for the serving girl who had already burned him.

ALEXEI

The closer to the sky you lived—the closer to the gods—the higher your status in Tal. The palace complex overlooked the city, and in the second highest building, on the seventh floor, slept the king. I had spent innumerable days up there as Dimi's rooms stood next to his father's, the extensive apartment filled with maps and knickknacks preferable to my own single room on the third floor. Only Dimi's influence had made the castle keeper house me that high. Now, in my effort to delay the inevitable confrontation with the Roja, I had sunk even lower. Not even the stable boys were made to sleep above the griffons.

The space I had selected was used for storage, the flying leathers and saddles rarely used in winter as it was even colder up in the skies than down here. I had swiped travel gear, including a blanket, from the next-door storage, and the well-built stone house kept out most of the chill while the fearful creatures below kept away unwanted visitors.

I had tried to ignore the clacking of their beaks and occasional shrill whistles, but they had merged with my dreams, giving the shadows who hunted me wings. Only once had Dimi been able to convince me to join him in the sky, and that had been one time too many.

Sighing, I counted the money in my remaining purse and hid half in my boot. There was no knowing when I would rashly decide to throw away the rest. My father had not sent funds since I reached adulthood and finished my education two years ago. Somehow, I would need to stand on my own feet while dodging prison and exile.

It was not the cracked ribs or hunger rumbling in my belly, but sickness at my own whining and the memory of Ansa's shining eyes that finally drove me from my hiding place. I would not break another promise. Whatever happened after, I could not let the Roja arrest me before keeping my word.

Despite washing in the palace bath and flirting with the laundress until she located the clothes I had dropped off before my life changed, nobles and servants alike gave me strange looks as I limped past. It was not public knowledge why Dimi had left in the middle of the night, and surely my beaten-up appearance would add to the rumors. I put my head down and hurried my steps. Would the Roja grab me out in the open? At least there was a healer who would not demand too many answers. Mariska knew as well as I what had happened to Dimi, as she had been in the temple that night and comforted Ekaterina afterward. Resolutely, I ignored the fact that I had spent the last month avoiding her.

I crossed the courtyard and gardens, passed the stable where I'd slept, and approached the tallest, and possibly oldest, building in Tal: the Women's Tower. The square structure had overlooked Tal since before the monarchy, when the high priestess of the Death Goddess ruled the city from the black monolith. It housed the noble women and children of Tal, and no man except the king could enter.

From arriving in the city at the age of six until turning twelve, I lived there, protected from anything worse than a tutor's ire.

Now, I entered one of the rooms built into the southern wall that protected the Tower's private gardens and rang a bell before settling to wait. Fire burned in the mosaic covered hearth, the black stone depicting the ziggurats and skeletons in the Temple District. I wondered yet again why over the centuries no one had replaced them with something more suitable for a man courting or father visiting his children and wife. Why did everything in Tal have to remind us of the dead drifting over the streets?

The door facing the Tower unlocked and a servant girl, surely no more than ten, entered. She froze when she saw me, her eyes widening at my blackened eye. The Tower was a proper place and I had become anything but.

"I fought two bears and lost," I said and winked, suppressing a wince and earning a shy smile in return.

She dared a step closer. "Were they big?"

"Giants." I painfully raised my arms, realizing it was not too far from the truth.

She giggled.

"Could you tell Mariska Radanova that Alexei Yurievich wishes to see her? Ask her to break fast with me. And tell her about the bears."

The girl nodded and left. Maybe the tales of my injuries would prepare Mariska for why I had come. One reason I had avoided her was that I did not want her to mistake my company for returned attraction. It did not help that I missed her animated face and the laughs we had shared. She had been the youngest in our quartet and I had taken her under my wing, teaching her my countryside ways—how to catch toads, make a reed whistle, and carve sticks.

The girl returned with tea, sweet-smelling breads stuffed with dried fruits, and *doleb* honey cookies. Before our table was arranged, Mariska entered. She had always been the smallest of us, and not just because of her age. At sixteen, she barely reached my shoulder. Her personality, buzzing with energy no matter the time of day, hands painting pictures as she talked, made her appear larger than the slip of a girl before me. With skin a shade darker than Dimi's golden one but the same black hair and sharp features, the familial resemblance was obvious despite their opposing temperaments.

Riska and I had seen each other only days ago at the interrupted wedding ceremony when everything broke, but it felt like we both had transformed. Her new coat, skirt, and blouse, all in healers' crimson, did not help. Seemed life was changing for all of us. Only full-time healers wore the red.

"You moving to the hospital?" I blurted out, forgetting the words I rehearsed on the way here. Even with the lack of healers, she had managed to put off the move. As she was third in line to the throne, few had argued.

Mariska waved the servant girl out and settled at the table. At least, as a full healer, we could meet alone without causing more rumors. An unexpected boon.

"It was that or remain in the Tower like Eki. I chose the hospital. It was anyway time." She studied me with cautious eyes. "Was it the king?"

I self-consciously touched my eye, then grinned. "Did you not hear about the bears?"

"You need someone to stand for you."

"It was just a brawl, Riska." Which did not mean she was wrong. "I'm considering leaving Tal."

"I could talk to my uncle. Dimi must be allowed back soon."

I shook my head and flinched as my left ribs moved in ways they definitely should not. Before I could object, Mariska was on her feet and pressed her palms against my cheeks in a too-intimate way.

The familiar tingling of healing lifted the hairs on my arms and swept the aches away while her eyes said too much.

As soon as the pain dissipated, I jumped to my feet. Being alone with her was a mistake. I could not lose one of the few genuine friends I had left. We all needed time. Time would fix everything.

"Alexei, I wanted to tell you—" Mariska said, and I did not wait to hear the end. She wanted someone to hold her through the storm, and it could not be me.

"Thank you for the healing, but I cannot stay." Two steps away from the open door and escape, I remembered my promise. Perhaps Mariska had heard of Ansa's future husband. "Do you know a Lord Siniy?"

"No." She took a step closer. "Don't leave yet."

I forced myself to meet her eyes. "We can't do this, Riska. I can't. We'll see each other soon."

I turned to escape and ran into the taller, broad-shouldered, male version of Mariska. We both staggered back before catching our balance. Nikolai, second in line to the throne and reputedly the most beautiful man in Tal, gave me an irate look. A few years our senior, he had already been out of the Tower, winning and breaking hearts, by the time I became old enough to look a woman's way. We were neither friends nor had any strife. And I needed no more problems.

Where Dimi was serious and dutiful, his older cousin was cavalier and used the royal privileges to live without care. His lavish parties were legendary and lovers scandalous. I might never want to marry, but I was a far cry from Nikolai Radanov.

His eyes, lined with dark lashes the ladies swooned over, narrowed as he looked from me to his little sister.

"Kola, Alexei just came to be healed," Mariska said before either of us could make it worse. "And he's leaving."

I nodded and stepped to the side with a half bow.

Nikolai did not move. "You asked about Lord Siniy? Stay away from him." He said the last more to his sister than me.

"You know him?" Mariska asked, and then to me, "What has he done?"

"I'm asking for a friend." I avoided her eyes, knowing she would not want to hear more. Though maybe if she thought me attached, things could return to normal between us.

Nikolai laughed without warmth. "If that's a female friend, tell her to run. I have never met the man. We don't move in the same circles. But social rules dictate I'm invited to all noble weddings—not that I go—and Siniy has sent invites to at least five which never took place. Rumors say the brides disappear before the ceremony."

"The man is probably a dreadful bore," Mariska said, and I exchanged a look with her brother. She had grown up in the Tower. Nikolai, Dimi, and I protected her when she was old enough for excursions. Maybe we had not done her any favors in keeping the ugliness of the world at bay.

I nodded to Nikolai. "I'll let my friend know."

"If you want the truth, ask von Uster." Nikolai hesitated, a shadow of his cousin's seriousness washing over him. "I'm sorry about

Dimi. If you want company, stop by the Jonava manor tonight. I'll make sure you're on the guest list."

I gave Nikolai another half bow, with a genuine smile in thanks this time, and left. Not to seek out Lord von Uster, royal spymaster and the head of the Roja. Even the suggestion showed that in some ways, Nikolai was as removed from the realities of life as his sister. If the king had any questions regarding my loyalties, von Uster would be the one to deliver the answers.

Thinking on my feet, I instead set out for the Archives, housed on 15 Crown Street, across Palace Road, which divided Tal's neighborhoods, and above the night market. Staying out of the palace seemed like a perfect idea, and no one would think to search for me among the dusty papers. All noble weddings were registered. It might take a day or two to dig through the documents, but surely Lord Siniy's marriage contracts would condemn or clear him.

Nikolai's vague warnings, the freezing winter winds, and the taste of snow hanging in the air sped my steps. One wedding ending in tears this winter because I stood by was enough.

CHAPTER FIVE

ANSA

I realized how tall Alexei was when I saw his head above the regulars at the bar, his amber eyes tracking me and a smile tugging at his lips. At least he did not try to catch my attention through another stunt. I waved for him to wait, despite wanting nothing more than to pelt him with questions about Siniy and noble life. But I could not afford to lose this job until the marriage contract was signed and Lanik's frown had not let up since I returned from the meeting at Popova's.

Each time I picked up an order, I snuck a look at the strange nobleman who had promised to help me, realizing I had not really expected him to return after I burned his wrist and, almost, the city.

I should have denied it when he claimed to owe me a debt, but the opportunity had been too good to pass up. The Wishmaker had brought him to me, and I needed information.

His russet skin told of ancestors from the Vsadnik steppe tribes and while he was tall and slender, he moved with force and did not stoop, owning his height. His arms had been strong around me, firm, until I moved away. He did not seem to realize that, despite my magic, he had truly saved me. If, after dropping the tray, I had accidentally shown the fire moving inside me here, the little say I had in my life would have evaporated. Someone would have wanted to use me. Tal was not at war but there were enough robbers outside the city and nobles clamoring for any advantage. Even they hid their magic from each other. Did Alexei have secret powers? Probably not, as he had taken the beating without displaying them.

As the orders slowed down, I convinced one of the other servers to take on my last tables as well. I would have to split my money, but Siniy's gold weighed heavily in my pocket, dragging me down. If I waited any longer to learn what Alexei knew, I might set the drink hall on fire.

He grinned as I approached, and before I could stop myself, I checked my hair. Having someone look at you like that was a too-easy way to lose focus. I carried one man's child and was marrying another. The last thing I needed was to care what a handsome stranger thought. It did not matter that his arms around me had been the most human contact I'd had since summer, three ever-colder and lonelier months ago.

"Did you find anything?" I asked as soon as I was within earshot, unable to hold back the question that had been screaming inside me since I saw him.

"Hi to you, too." Alexei glanced at Lanik, standing behind the bar close enough to overhear. "I've something that could end up being nothing. Or something. Do you want to talk here?"

No. I did not want my work to know of my secret pregnancy, magic, and arranged marriage. I should not even have approached Alexei so openly. I was not normally this rash. Either Alexei's carefree smile or the babe in my belly had made me momentarily forget where I was. It could not happen again.

"I know a barge still open in winter. We can speak there," I said, and gave Lanik a hard look. "It's well frequented." *So don't try to rob us again.*

But Lanik did not even look my way. Instead, the already pale man seemed to have lost all his blood at Alexei's cutting grin. Turned to me, it had appeared easygoing, but not so when aimed at my boss. Guess he had figured out who had ratted on us. Lanik, seeing Alexei's fine clothes, would think him the fire bearer and probably worried the noble had returned to burn the drink hall to the ground. I both wished to spill the truth to gain some of that respect, and declare Alexei the crown prince's companion and mage, and see Lanik faint.

At least I was still sensible enough to do neither.

This time, I accepted Alexei's offered arm without hesitation, already trusting enough to follow where he led, though the past should have taught me not to. Together, we exited into the twilight.

"Your Lord Siniy is a hard man to find."

I leaned closer, sharing my warmth as the icy wind pushed against us. "Tell me."

"No one I know seems to have met the man and the only thing they have heard about him relates to his unmatched wealth and many broken engagements, each greatly celebrated."

"I agreed to marry him this morning," I confessed.

Alexei stopped in the middle of the street, pedestrians behind cursing before moving around us. He faced me, the concern in his eyes telling me he knew more than he had said. "Congratulations?"

"I had no choice. I need a husband. Fast."

"And if I found something objectionable?"

I pulled at him to resume our walk. How could I tell this man I barely knew how foolish I had been? Or explain why I wanted to keep the child? How giving it up or stopping the pregnancy would be accepting Mother's rejection of me. Since living on my own, I had imagined what kind of mother I would be. How I would be better than her. How could I fail the first time I was put to the test? For once, the fire could be what saved us both.

The silence stretched until we arrived at the orange-painted party barge floating on the Taliell. In summer, barges covered the river's many arms, and the dancing, drinking, and plays lasted until the sun rose. During winter, most barges were covered to protect the bright paint from the weather and patrons from falling off the often rain-slick or iced-over decks. This one, The Sunrise, never closed and before my pregnancy, I often visited with my fair-weather friends after work to dance and drink.

If I straightened my back and painted a smile on my face as we entered in case someone saw me on the arm of a handsome, well-to-do man and drew the wrong conclusions, no one could blame me. I wanted nothing more than for that simple image to be true.

Colorful lanterns illuminated the night as we settled by one of the nailed down tables. At the end of the barge, the dance floor stood abandoned and open to the sky, but here, fraying awnings hung to hold off sun and rain.

Alexei waved down a server and ordered tea and hotcakes. I wanted to object that I could take care of myself, but we both knew that despite his protestations about what kind of noble he was, anyone living in the palace had resources a Lowtown denizen would never match.

When alone again, I gathered my courage. "Knowing is better than not, no matter what."

He squeezed my hand, and it felt so natural. No expectations. No pressure. And, despite knowing what I was, no fear.

"I visited the Archive to separate truth from rumor. It took a while to find what I was looking for."

"They just let you in?"

He shrugged. "Despite what you saw the other night, I can be very persuasive. And I might have claimed you were my little sister."

"Did you now?" Part of me *really* did not want to be his sister, because his chilly hand in my too-warm one was not brotherly. I should not have cared. The concern in his eyes should not have raised my pulse and heated the winter air around us.

"They were very helpful. You might also have been blind and fifteen, locked up by our parents. Don't look at me like that. There was a lot of dust to sort through and each time they wanted me to leave, I had to make our cause more desperate."

I laughed despite waiting to hear what felt like my doom. "You like to lay it on thick. Now stop delaying."

"As the lady demands. First, I looked through marriage contracts and found two with Lord Rostya of House Siniy as the groom, one from ten years ago, the second one eight years ago. You mentioned he had previous wives, so not suspicious in itself. Engagement contracts are only kept until the wedding, or dissolution of the agreement. Still, I found one from two years ago. The archivists claimed it must have been missed in the last purge."

"So, I would be his fourth bride?"

"At least. There's no way of knowing."

"Three wives are unusual but not too strange for a man his age." Maybe his fascination with my magic, something I had been taught to hide, had colored my impression of him.

Alexei nodded. "I planned to leave it at that yesterday, then one of the archivists, now invested in easing your final days—"

"I'm dying?"

"I might have thrown in a disease or two. Anyway, she suggested we check the death certificates to ensure the previous Ladies Siniy had indeed died. Apparently, it happens that rich lords marry more than one woman and keep them in separate manors. A private man like Siniy could easily do such a thing."

I nodded apprehensively, having not even considered this. "And did he?"

"No. The ladies are all dead, so your marriage would be legal." Alexei squeezed my hand. "They both died the day after their weddings."

"What?"

"We matched the dates on the marriage contracts with the death certificates. The previous Ladies Siniy each held the title a single day."

His words hung in the air as the server brought our order. Alexei paid. I barely noticed. My chest tingled. Mouth dried. The air heated. *What natural explanation could there be for two women, two years apart, to die the day after marrying?*

"Did they leave inheritances?" At least if it was about money, I would be safe, for I had none.

"Both came from minor noble families. It could have been a jealous lover. A servant since dismissed. One could have run away, and he declared her dead to save face."

"Or it could have been the lord."

The air rippled. Black scorch marks spiraled out from my free hand across the wooden table. I needed to breathe, but the fire inside was eating the air.

Alexei slid over to my side of the table and wrapped his long arms around me again. He stroked my cheek, and the caring fingers distracted me. But the memory of drowning, of being an uncontrollable monster, lay too close to the surface. Sweat stuck the dress to my skin, air coming in gulps. I squished my eyes closed, grasping for control.

"Stay with me," Alexei said, tilting my head until our eyes met. He was beautiful despite the crooked nose and unkempt hair, holding me like I mattered. He did not see a monster. I pressed even closer, desperate to stay in the moment.

We sat on the barge, rain pattering on the awning above, and I wished we were the last people in the world. I barely knew him. Had met him twice and lost control both times, and still, his clean scent spoke of safety in the storm that was my life. The fire, already loose inside me, twisted into something else. I wet my lips, knowing I should pull away. Knowing nothing could come of this.

His eyes traveled to my mouth as he brushed a stray hair from my forehead. "Were you not marrying another, Ansa, I would treat you as anything but sisterly. I might not desire marriage, but I respect it enough to know my place." His face softened. "I don't know why you're marrying a man you clearly don't know—and you don't have to tell me. I am just a stranger wishing you to remain safe."

The truth leaped from my tongue, bypassing my brain.

"I'm pregnant."

His arms tensed around me. "And the father?"

I sighed. "I was so stupid, thinking the dreams he spun would come true. He's a merchant with one of the summer caravans from Sorach. He played me a fool and left Tal and me as soon as the season turned. Only a month later did I even suspect I carried a child."

"Sharing yourself with someone you cared for while trusting their word isn't stupid. Or if it is, it is a stupidity we have all committed—some too many times."

His lips twisted, and I could imagine all the women who had listened to his sweet words and let him into their beds.

"Stupid or not, it means I need a husband. My child a father."

"Does Siniy know?"

I looked away, refusing to see the pity. "That's why he wants me. The father is also a fire bearer."

Alexei let out a low whistle. "A foreign mage. Your child will be blessed. Few know how rare magic has become in Tal."

"Even among the nobles?" I dared to look back and found only interest in his eyes.

"I have none. The stories that all nobles possess magic might have once been true. Too many died in the last plague outbreaks, and more since. Dimi—my friend—knew the truth and told me. In Tal, magic is dying."

Dimitri Alexandre Ivanov. Alexei really had gone from spending his time with the crown prince to me. He had probably been taught of the world, knew things I could not imagine, still I could not let his words stand.

"Fire is not a blessing, only a curse," I said. "I've hid it all my life. I want my child trained and safe. A commoner with magic is an aberration to be used, a noble someone to be treasured."

"Don't you have family who can help?"

I only shook my head, and he did not press.

After a moment of silence, I sighed. "At least if Siniy had something to do with the deaths of his wives, he will want me alive until my child is born."

Alexei tensed around me. "No one is killing you. I have no money, standing or mage training, or I would offer you the use of it all."

I laughed it off. It was easy to offer when you had nothing to give. He had already more than repaid anything he owed me.

"It's probably not true, anyway. Anything could have happened all those years ago. Maybe he offended the Death Goddess, and she came to collect."

Alexei held me tight, though I was not sure he noticed. "I have one more person I can ask. Don't sign the marriage contract yet."

I could make no promises, so instead stared at the wet dance floor, remembering easier times. Alexei followed my gaze and seemed to shake off the morose mood as if it was a coat he could change when it did not suit.

"Do you need to go back to work? Before you become a lady, you should see what you have to expect, and you're not married yet. I have an invitation to the party of the night, and would be honored if you, Ansa, my blind, diseased sister, came as my companion."

I should have said no. It was the sensible thing to do. But I could too well imagine spending the night worrying about the future, and then worrying my worrying would set the bed on fire. Another woman might have gone to the temple and prayed to the Goddess to pass her by. Instead, my lips mirrored his, and I nodded.

His eyes twinkled golden. "I only ask one favor of you."

"What?"

"That you let down your hair."

Without looking away, I pulled out the pins securing my bun one by one. "Show me a night of living."

Ansa

Alexei took me to the arcade which divided the night market from Crown Street. Even in the winter drizzle, people squeezed past, their bright-colored coats and fur-lined hoods dotting the night. Stores spilled out between the arcade's columns, each one ladened with fine wares and guarded over by a junior shop attendant, often hardly more than a child.

Between tables displaying mechanical contraptions from the coastal cities and gloves which seemed too fine to wear, a boy waved dresses and coats for rent. We pushed past the outer tables filled with fabric and entered the warm, narrow store. Despite my protestations over the cost, Alexei and the female shop assistant helped me select an ankle-length dress they swore was fitting for a party. Siniy's gold lay heavy in my pocket. I should have offered to pay, but spending the money would make it real. Keeping it I could pretend I still had options.

As the assistant tightened the corset until I could no longer bend, I could not deny the beautiful figure I saw in the mirror. The deep green set off my loose red hair like my normal white, gray, and black never did, and the wide skirts, with more fabric than I could ever afford, swished between my legs as I moved. I had spent so many years trying to not draw attention, to hide everything that made me unique, that I hardly recognized the smiling face reflected back at me. The woman then offered me a short evening cloak to complete the fashionable winter look, and I accepted despite not feeling the cold air.

As I exited the dressing area, Alexei looked me up and down with a lascivious glint as his bright eyes snagged on my bare collarbone.

"The lady requires a necklace as well, I think."

The shop owner, a dark-skinned man with bushy eyebrows seated behind the counter, cleared his throat. His pinched lips as he studied me indicated a less than flattering opinion. He then looked at the money Alexei had already placed before him, as you needed proof of payment before touching the garments.

"The coin will not cover the security for any of our fine jewelry," the store owner said. "The simplest one would require triple the money just for the deposit."

I balked. That was nearly all the money Siniy had given me. "Don't be rash. It's already too much," I stammered.

"We both deserve a night of fun. Believe me when I say I have made much rasher decisions. And I'll get it back." Alexei removed the ring from his finger and placed it on the counter. "This should be enough collateral for everything."

"But what if I—"

He placed a hand on my shoulder. "If you truly don't want it, we can leave now. But I trust you. Just return it in the morning and there will be no issue."

The owner examined the ring while the assistant selected a gold-plated necklace for me.

"This is yours?" the old man finally asked, implying neither of us should possess such a ring.

Alexei rolled up his sleeve, revealing the noble's sigil over now unblemished skin. He might call himself poor, but anyone who could see a healer for something as small as a burn lived in a different world than me. Marrying Siniy could change that.

"I apologize, my lord," the owner said with a light bow, his whole demeanor transforming. "Would there be anything else?"

Alexei looked at me, and I shook my head. It was already too much. Who spent so frivolously on a stranger?

Outside, the icy rain had halted and the constant wind calmed. The street was even fuller, the market and stores doing good business despite the season.

Alexei offered me his arm. "Do you feel like walking? The party should be on the edge of North's Place."

"No need to spend any more. Luckily, I still have my own shoes." I wiggled my toes in the sturdy leather boots.

As we strolled, merchants called out to draw our attention to their wares. Others nodded in respect I never received in my own clothes. It was the same streets, the same people, but walking it as a well-to-do woman on the arm of a respectable man was a different world. Something inside me, a hardness I had not been aware of, relaxed a fraction. There was no need to fidget with my clothes or hair to make the little I had pass inspection, like armor hiding my strangeness. Even the fire calmed, as if it felt me relax.

Alexei bent to bring our heads closer. "It wasn't all made up. I have a sister and she's not well." He touched the edge of the fine dress fabric where it brushed against his pants. "Zora would have loved this, loved Tal, but the travel would be too much for her. I haven't seen her for a year."

"Why are you telling me?"

He smiled. "You asked why I would spend the night like this. You made me think of her, and then how I might see her soon. I'll tell her of you and this little adventure. It would make her smile. If I don't come up with something, I'll be forced to return to my family."

"Would that be so bad?"

Alexei swept his arm, taking in the merchants and the busy Palace Road we were approaching. "And leave all this?"

I saw dirty streets, rushing people, the poor begging in alley mouths and knew the stench of piss that would greet you inside. Pocket-thieving children stalked the few nobles deigning to walk the streets while laborers drew carts filled with food, drink, and wares from Gateways to Midtown and Rivertown.

"Isn't the countryside peaceful and safe?"

"Very much so." Alexei pulled me even closer to allow a coach to pass before continuing. I did not mind nearly as much as I should have that he had not let me go since the barge. "And every day there is the same," Alexei continued, "including the people. I miss some, but a month a year is enough—the conversations and complaints never change. The harvest, weather and sales prices. Issues with the tribes and trade with Tal. If you're lucky, someone in Denyev married or performed an act worthy of a bit of gossip."

I had never left the city, knew nothing besides the lorists and travelers' tales. Still, his description felt lacking. "But isn't it beautiful?"

He shrugged. "The only thing that changes are the seasons. Tal, even in its ugliness, hides wonder. Things to experience and figure out. Stories, each one more unbelievable than the next."

"That's because they're not true."

We paused, watching the hectic Palace Road with coaches and runners rushing up and down.

"Finding the truth is what makes it interesting." Quieter, he said, "I owe it all to Dimi. When I arrived, I was the country kid whose only skill was climbing trees and still thought I knew everything. He taught me about life here, allowed me to join his lessons, while I mostly got him into trouble. Now he's in the biggest trouble of his life, and where am I?"

With a jerk, he pulled us forward between the speeding carriages as if to stop me from questioning his words. The coach drivers cursed but we were already away, weaving through the traffic. At each near miss, my skin heated further, threatening to damage the rented clothes.

As we passed the last one and leapt onto the courthouse steps on the other side, Alexei grinned again, his hair tousled and cheeks heated. Torn between cursing and kissing him, I closed my eyes and stilled my center. Was the babe making the magic less pliant or was the stress getting to me? I had gone most of my life without incidents and now it always burned under the surface, ready to incinerate everything.

A hand brushed my cheek, and I looked into bright playful eyes. Had I ever been that carefree? I retreated a step.

"Don't do that again." The words were supposed to be angry but came out weak and small. Not sure if I meant the soft touch or mad dash, I took another step back. "This was a bad idea."

He looked like he wanted to argue, but instead, he offered me his arm like a gentleman. "One more block and we will be inside. I promise no more running."

I had the dress and necklace. Had come this far. Despite my churning gut, I placed my hand on the offered arm, and he steered me into North's Place.

The houses became progressively finer, gardens grander, and streetlamps brighter. Despite the slowing foot traffic, it was clean and safe, and the patrolling city guards in their bone gray coats nodded politely as they passed us by.

We stopped only two blocks in, an intricate iron gate open to showcase a hundred lanterns in covered flower beds. The manor behind them was three floors of palest pink, like the finest confectionery. Ladies and lords spilled out from the wide-open doors and leaned out the windows. Somewhere inside, musicians played a mournful tune, contrasting against the raucous laughs. My hands clenched around Alexei's arm. I had never been anywhere remotely similar. I might torch it due to nerves if I did not calm. It felt like everyone watched me, like they could read my secrets on my exposed skin.

As he led me up the stairs, Alexei, fitting in without trying, nodded to the milling couples. Before I could decide on the appropriate greeting—*do I nod? Bow?*—we were inside and I dared to breathe again.

Lanterns draped in dark-purple cloth barely illuminated the soaring entry, and polished stone floors that should have reflected the ten-armed chandelier above somehow ate the light. Instead of a servant, a round table stacked with fine bottles and thin-stemmed glasses, the kind that would not survive a night in Rivertown, greeted us.

Alexei offered me a glass and grabbed one for himself, raising it with a grin. The women next to us lifted their own in answer. With a cheer, they called, "For Tal. For all," then emptied their glasses, Alexei following, while I tentatively sipped the pink liquid. Bubbles popped on my tongue and sweetness followed. Around us, finely dressed nobles and rich merchants laughed and shouted to each other. Through the next doors, couples of any gender danced together, and not the formal kind. The music was louder than outside, encouraging my body to sway in time.

"Do you like it?" Alexei asked, pressing closer to be heard. "Nikolai always delivers on a party."

I watched the roaring crowd, so different from the reserved nobles on the street. Before Alexei, I had not even spoken to one. It was chaos and beauty and excess. At the Drunken Dead, no one worried about tomorrow because they could not change it. Had already given up. Here, they did not worry because it was already secured. If they fell, they knew the world would catch them. If something broke, they would purchase its replacement without counting the pennies and worries. Marrying Siniy, despite Alexei's warnings, took on a shine as golden as the coins he had given me. I could soon be one of these carefree creatures.

I raised my glass to Alexei and sipped again, murmuring, "For Tal. For all." Around me, everyone cheered.

We danced and ate, and while Alexei waved to others, his attention remained fixed on me, his fingers playing with my loose hair or resting on my hip as the alcohol painted ruddy roses on his cheeks. The music became more sensual, pushing us closer. Despite not drinking more, I burned deliciously in his arms; the constant fear whisked away together with my worries.

Alexei mumbled something about seeking the privy, which was what the rich called the outhouse apparently, and I realized I also had to go. He left me with a group of colorful ladies waiting around plush sofas surrounded by mirrors. I abandoned my tired legs and sat, stroking the velvet.

Next to me, the dark-skinned beauty in a dress covering barely half of her skin leaned closer.

"You came with Lord Yurievich—Alexei? He's a treat, isn't he?" She winked and I could not suppress my smile.

"I'm having a great time."

"I'm so glad to see him out and about after what happened. The prince disappearing like that. Who would have thought…" She smiled indulgently. "I guess a good party takes the pressure of an uncertain future. What's your name? I don't believe we've met."

I squirmed under her calculating eyes. "What do you mean uncertain future?"

She waved a hand that had never seen a day's labor as if swatting a fly. "With the prince gone. Last year, Alexei and I had our own little tryst, but I would never risk it now." Her teeth gleamed as she raised her voice. "I'm *so glad* he found someone."

The two women standing next to us paused their conversation and followed her gaze to me. "Oh, Alexei is a treat, isn't he?"

I could not stop the blush creeping up my cheeks nor the churning in my belly. I had no right to him. Still, the knowing smiles around me dug like claws. He had said there was no shame in enjoying another's body. It seemed he took that literally.

"It's not like that," I mumbled, and was saved by the ladies' privy door opening, providing me with an escape.

At least their shit smelled no better than any poor outhouse. Somehow, that centered me. Under the clothes they were all the same, though under mine rolled fire. Even sitting here alone, uncomfortable jealousy threatened scorch marks to the fine wood.

I delayed inside until someone knocked on the door a third time. *Open, find Alexei, and say it's time to leave,* I told myself.

Everything was fine. I had forgotten myself in this fairy tale, but it was not for me. I needed calm. *Peace.* Could Siniy give me that? Did it matter what secrets he hid from years ago when he had asked for none of mine?

I left with a sigh and was greeted by an intoxicated, irate woman with hair tumbling down to her behind. She pushed past me and slammed the door closed, leaving me facing the lady who had spoken to me. Did she spend the whole party here, ready to ambush and stir trouble? A tiny, younger woman in a healer-red dress, but without the distinct coat, sat next to her talking animatedly, hands and hair wild. Then my attention snapped to Alexei, who was quickly closing the distance on his long legs, and the air came easier. Already he seemed like a safe harbor.

"There you are," he said almost at my side, while at the same time, the petite healer leaped to her feet.

"Alexei," she exclaimed. "Kola said you were coming. We could get a drink and talk."

She was already halfway to him on unsteady legs. He seemed to speed up even more.

The dark beauty smiled like this was an unexpected treat, and said, "He's actually here with someone." The healer's face fell. They all now stared at me.

"It's not like that," I said again, wishing I could disappear. A noble's displeasure could see you hung. The fire and anxiety fed each other, the claws inside tearing. The healer's face lit up at my words, her brilliant smile clearly meant for Alexei. He saw it, panic flashing in his eyes, then he held me in his arms—but not the way he had when we were alone.

"It's just like that," he claimed, and before I could react, closed the distance between our lips.

Fire shot through my blood, fighting to escape as I instinctively clung to his shirt, tasting wine and him, until my mind caught up and I pushed him away.

We stared at each other, the moment hanging frozen in the air, until the dark beauty's laugh snapped me back to our surroundings.

They all saw.

The walls closed in. The music, no longer calming and seductive, overwhelmed my thoughts. My lips pressed together despite my lungs screaming for air.

I pushed past Alexei and ran blindly through the rooms, uncaring who I offended. I needed to get away. My hand scorched a wall, barely missing the heavy curtains. I clenched my fists, blanking my mind until the icy air hit me in the face. Collapsing against the side of the house, I gulped it down. The cold winter night and light drizzle had driven everyone else inside.

Why did I keep letting people use me? Tiredness swept through me—of always being on guard, of fighting so long I no longer knew what was right, of fearing part of myself.

The candles in the lanterns had burned low, barely illuminating Alexei's tall shape as he approached. At least he had the sense to stop outside my reach.

"I didn't mean to offend you. It was just a kiss," he said, and I could hear the chagrin in his voice. "You didn't have to run."

"Would you have preferred me burning down the house?" Anger and fire rose again, sparks flickering between my fingers. "You kissed me in front of all of them. To make a point. I'm engaged. What if they know Siniy? What if they come to my wedding? How can I face anyone?"

"You're still marrying him after what I told you?"

I hit the wall behind me with flaming hands, loose hair blowing in my face. My control was slipping. Life unraveling. Be it the babe or the events, I had to stop. Find somewhere to hide away from the world. "What choice do I have? You kiss me and claim me in front of everyone. Do *you* want to follow through?"

He dared a step closer despite the flames, and I could see the confusion on his face. "Ansa, I have nothing to offer besides a good time. I never desired marriage or children. I've already sworn my life to someone and let him down."

"That's right. Seemed several in there have enjoyed your *good time*. At least Siniy hasn't disrespected me yet, treated me like a courtesan to dress up and enjoy, for everyone to watch and talk about."

His face hardened. "It's not like that and you know it. If you want to be a noble, you should get used to rumors. No one trusts them, and you won't be anywhere close to the top of things talked about after this party."

I knew he was probably right. That he had invited me without bad intentions. But his kiss still burned on my too-hot lips, the fire lit my blood, and it was all too much.

"Not everyone can choose good times and not care about other's judgments. You say you have nothing, but you're just spoiled. You're too far removed to know what *nothing* means."

He came even closer, caging me with his arms. Surely, he felt the heat emanating from my body. "You have no idea what it's like to be branded with a sigil from birth, knowing your choices can be overridden. That you're trapped. Especially in a family where you do not belong."

My too-fast breaths mixed with his and I voiced truths I worked a lifetime to suppress. "I don't know what it's like to not belong? When I was five, I burned my sister's arm in anger, and to protect *the family*, my mother tried to drown me in the Taliell. You've no idea what it's like to know you're too dangerous to ever relax. Marrying isn't some fancy or for advantage. It's safety and companionship. Stability. You jeopardized *everything*."

I spit the last word in his shocked face.

"Ansa…"

Ignoring his pleading tone, I pushed on. This thing we started had to stop. "Your life doesn't seem that bad anymore?"

He lowered his angry voice. "The money from my family could send would hardly cover room and board. I owe everything I have to Dimi. The clothes on my back, the teaching I received, the doors that open for me. Even the invite to the party tonight. Due to him I could afford to make my own decisions, and while he asked for nothing in return, I swore him my life."

"Then you're already married, just not to a woman. You've shown what it means to be a noble and not care about consequences. The lady in there asked about your prince. Perhaps you should worry more about your own life and less about mine."

I tore out of his arms and walked into the night in a dress not my own, clenching my hands to suffocate the flames as the first snow of the year fell around me. When I looked back, Alexei was gone.

ALEXEI

I stumbled back to the palace through the pure snow as dawn tinged the sky and Spirits evaporated. The night was supposed to have been a fun distraction, an impulse that allowed us both to escape our current situations for a moment. Holding her on the barge after delivering my findings, I had longed to stretch the night for after I delivered on my debt there was no longer a reason to meet again.

It had been a twirl of colors and time spent making Ansa laugh. I had kept us to the main areas where clothes still were mandatory and senses less impaired, but even there, lords and ladies who usually judged anyone who stepped out of line let go, as I had thought Ansa needed to.

It was perfect until I, like an idiot riding the wave of drink and touch, saw Mariska coming with stars in her eyes. I panicked. Badly. But I had wanted to kiss Ansa since I laid eyes on her. The spark that lit me up as our lips touched had been no more a lie than how we had danced ever closer.

My feet took me back to my own room; I did not have the energy to seek another bed. Surely, no one could be watching all the time. And if they were, I was too tired to care.

I fell asleep still dressed, Ansa's damning words echoing in my mind. One thing she had gotten right: there was no more time for distractions or using others to avoid my problems. I could not live waiting for the ax to fall. I needed to face the king's judgment and make the best of the situation—before I got myself into even more trouble hiding from it. I needed to be in a position to help Dimi get his revenge when he returned. For after hearing his rage and grief as his father ordered him into exile, I had no doubt my friend would seek it.

After a few bells of sleep, I awoke with a pounding headache to a knock as a letter emblazed with my family sigils slid under my door. It must have been sent by griffon at an exorbitant cost to reach me already. Seemed the news had traveled to my mother faster than I had anticipated, as if the world itself conspired to make me face my problems. Worse, somehow, someone knew I was here. The ever-ticking, finely crafted clock in the corner, a gift from Dimi on my name day, reminded me time was running out with each pendulum swing. Ansa could look after herself. She was probably better at it than me anyway.

I wanted nothing more than to throw the letter into a drawer and forget the summons it was bound to contain. Instead, I clenched it tight. No matter how well I could predict the content, it would haunt me until I read it. And I had just decided to face my problems. Seemed this would be the first test.

A flick of my finger broke the sigil—a magic one, the cost even higher than the speedy delivery—and prepared for my mother's careful words. Instead, the harsh scrawl of the man I knew as my father greeted me. I skimmed it once. Then read it carefully. Twice. It did not change.

What I got right: Without the advantage of influence over our next ruler, my father would not pay even a meagre stipend until I got on my feet. Instead, he called me home to help manage the manor, ancestral lands, and apple orchards. Thankfully, as he was not the Head of our House, he could only ask. Still, my noble sigil seemed to itch. However, these were not the parts that made me reread.

What I got wrong: My brother, a decade my senior and a copy of my father, remained childless despite years of marriage. We all knew my sister, often bound to a wheelchair, was not expected to marry. Now, my father's health was declining and distant cousins were circling, debating how to best divvy up the land he loved. He begged me to come home and marry. As long as my children were raised on the estate, he promised they would inherit it all.

He signed it with his love.

I read the final words a fourth time and tried to imagine the hard man I knew begging. Or express *love*.

While it raised my heart, it seemed too absurd, and quiet country living, marriage, and managing the lands, felt barely better than the prison cell I feared. For my mother and sister, I would visit, but not since the first year had I ever wished to extend my time there. That did not change that even this small room would soon be beyond my means. I had been trained in languages, geography, and fighting. Court politics and dances. But I was in the king's bad graces and thus probably unemployable. Perhaps I could leave for one of the coastal cities, or Oberwalden high in the mountains, and learn to love another city. Everything inside me rejected the idea. No matter how broken it was, my life was in Tal.

As I dressed, my empty ring finger reminded me of last night. Another irresponsible failure. My sigil ring remained in a Midtown shop waiting for a dress and necklace I had no way of retrieving. Perhaps I could inquire at the Drunken Dead tonight. Would Ansa still be there? She had not known when Siniy would come to collect her, but I could not imagine he would give her time to reconsider—if a woman like that chose me, I would never let her go. If I was looking to settle down, that was. *Which I'm not*, I reminded myself, and threw the letter on the desk. It was already messing with my mind by offering the parental approval I had desired as a child in exchange for my freedom and duty to Dimi.

I had things to take care of today. First, my potential treason charges, then, if still free, Mariska. I had been avoiding her to spare her feelings but from how her face fell last night, I was doing anything but, and when I returned inside, I had been unable to find her. It had reminded me I had too few people in my life to push away those I held dear.

Still bleary-eyed, I made it to the main hall to break fast together with the majority of the palace's residents. Better to confront my problems in public. If needed, I would come quietly and it might give me an opportunity to argue my case. At least the king was rarely seen outside banquets and court. I was seeking someone else. The man who knew everything, and I had been determined to avoid.

While decimating an apple, and not questioning why I had selected something that reminded me of the orchards at Sizov, I leaned against a back wall and surveyed the bustling hall.

The higher your status, the closer to the currently empty dais you ate. The man I sought had the right to press against it. No one would question the head of the Roja as he whispered into the king's ear. Still, I focused on the people in the middle of the room where status was less strict. Lower nobles such as me mixed with black-coated army captains, and ladies in ruby, emerald, and sapphire winter dresses chatted over tea. Lord von Uster had a reputation for knowing everything and showing up in unexpected places. He would be easily overlooked, quietly overhearing gossip and secrets.

There.

The man's wrinkled skin seemed sun-kissed even in winter, his hair completely white. He sat close to the garden windows, seeming to unobtrusively soak in the cold sunlight. Despite his small size, I feared him more than I had the giant laborers ready to stomp my head in the alley a few days ago. There, I had a chance, however slim; here, the judgment had already been made, and I was stepping up to receive the sentence. My eyes jumped around the room, seeking any distraction just as Ansa had accused me of.

Before my courage could falter, von Uster's eyes snapped open, as if he had felt my approach. It was well possible he had somehow known I was here. There had been quiet rumors since I arrived in Tal of the powers he might possess—unconfirmed, for no one spoke loudly of magic. If I thought the king would allow a mind witch in his court, I would have suspected von Uster able to read my mind. Instead, his raised eyebrow as I stopped before him probably indicated an educated guess.

I finished the last of the apple, chewing hard to busy myself and hide my apprehension.

"Spit it out then," von Uster snapped.

"What?" Had I not swallowed, I would have choked. Or obeyed in pure reflex and spit apple remnants on the spymaster.

"Why you're here interrupting my morning. If I were you, I would not make more of a nuisance of myself than I already had. You're lucky we arrived in time to stop the prince, or you would no longer have been able to come and pester me. Don't question the Wishmaker's blessing or king's decision."

"I'm safe?"

Von Uster nodded briskly. "The less spoken about it, the better. Your disappearance would only add to the rumors. You've made too much of a show of yourself over the years to go quietly now. The king's orders are that it never happened. Can you hold your tongue?"

"Always."

The wound-up coil inside me relaxed. Even the headache from last night's drink subsided. Though, my financial troubles and the appeal to return home remained. Dimi was still gone, and I had no role at court, but I could stop looking over my shoulder. My fate was in my own hands. Much like Ansa's was in hers, and she was risking it all to secure a future. As my fear subsided, her other words rose through the fog of drink. Her mother had tried to *kill her*. I did not owe her anything but when I came begging for the dress and necklace, it might go better if I had more information to offer. And maybe if I knew she was safe, the nagging guilt in the back of my mind would ease.

Von Uster waved impatiently for me to go. Nikolai had told me that if anyone knew of Siniy, it was the man before me. Ignoring the part of me screaming to leave while I was ahead, I took the chair opposite the spymaster, though I did not go as far as reaching for one of the perfect confections arranged on the middle of the table.

The old man stiffened, but something like interest sparkled in his eyes. For the first time, I seemed to have his full attention.

"Yes?"

"A friend of mine is marrying Lord Siniy. I only need to know if he is a good man, and you know everyone's secrets. The deaths of his previous wives... please." I swallowed, remembering my impulsive kiss and the fire she suppressed, thinking only of not hurting anyone else. "Despite what you might think of me, she only deserves good."

"So, you know about the wives. Through the rumors and records, I assume. How many did you find?"

Ice filled me at the casual question. "Two marriages and one engagement. Nikolai led me to believe there might have been more."

"Noble engagements must be announced to the crown as the king, though he rarely does, can refuse his blessing, and I, of course, keep track," von Uster said, and I leaned forward to not miss a word. "I've been curious for years what Siniy does with them, but there have always been higher priorities and no evidence of wrongdoing. I assumed that's why they started disappearing before signing the marriage contract. Less of a paper trail. I know of at least seven."

Blood drained from my face, Ansa's smile as we danced shining inside me. "Seven dead brides?"

Von Uster nodded. "As far as I can tell. I would advise your friend to break the engagement before it is announced."

"No families ever sought justice?"

"I assume a man such as him knows how to select the right bride."

Ansa was desperate enough not to ask questions. She had been abandoned by her family and the father of her child. And I had let her walk away.

I jumped to my feet, barely catching the chair before it clattered to the floor.

Von Uster raised an eyebrow. "If you find the evidence, consider it a sanctioned arrest. You have my blessing to make him pay. If you find nothing, you are on your own."

I hardly heard him. Ansa could not become the eighth.

My long legs covered the distance of the hall, my mind blanking as I, again, ran straight into Nikolai Radanov. I had not seen the man for months, and now it seemed I could not escape him. Social protocol demanded morning greetings and well-wishes, but I had time for neither.

As soon as the prince opened his mouth, I snapped, "Not now."

"That's the thanks I get after the good time I heard you had last night?"

I was already leaving.

"I came to find you." He called after me and waved a paper in the air. "My morning mail contained another engagement ball invitation to Lord Siniy and the soon-to-be Lady Siniy. The party is tonight, the wedding—a smaller affair, even I not invited—tomorrow."

I froze in horror. I was already too late.

CHAPTER EIGHT

ANSA

After trudging through the white flakes, my steps the first to break the perfection, I arrived at my rented room on 15 Ulna Street, at the border between Rivertown and Lowtown, only to discover the fire under my skin made it impossible to sleep. It churned hotter and hotter as images and touches from the party haunted me.

When sleep finally found me bells later, memories mixed with dark figures pulling me down, screaming I was too dangerous to live, while I ran toward amber eyes that kept turning away.

The morning found me sweat drenched, and no more rested. Normally, I would sleep until midday and then get ready for work. Perhaps it was the corset I still wore, perhaps a sense of premonition, or frustrations from last night, that pushed me to ready myself before the sun was halfway up the sky. I would return the dress and be done with it all.

I did not get the chance. Before I had even changed into my own clothes, Odilia herself—my standoffish landlady—entered with a firm knock and announced Siniy's coach had arrived to take me directly to my new home. Odilia watched as a flurry of servants who bowed without meeting my eyes packed my few possessions, while I was directed to go ahead. Our lord was expecting me, and even after two years under her roof, Odilia sent me off without comment.

The questions Alexei had raised about Siniy's previous wives swirled in my mind, kept back by my stiff smile. I could not start my new life by making a fool out of myself. Either it was nothing or his servants would not tell a future wife—especially not one on the verge of running.

With a deep breath, straight skirt, and pinned hair, still in rented clothes, I stepped into the finest carriage I had ever seen. The red velvet seat cushioned our passage from Lowtown's white streets, over Rivertown's bridges, past the now-empty night market, and across the busy Palace Road. Thus we traveled from southern to northern Tal, from poor to rich, packed streets to the sprawling gardens and estates of North's Place. Snow covered everything, as if trying to hide the inequalities, but nothing could disguise how houses grew larger and people fewer.

Ladies in emerald coats walked shadowed by pale-dressed servants. Even a griffon passed us, its great wing feathers and sharp beak catching the sunlight escaping through the cloud cover. It was the closest I had ever gotten to one of the fearful creatures bred for the skies and mountains. Did Alexei ride one? Until recently, I believed all nobles possessed magic and flew, but I could not imagine Siniy in leathers soaring through the sky. The image of Alexei in a similar position was harder to dismiss. Last night, in his arms among laughing ladies and lords who assumed I belonged, I had savored how his eyes never left mine. *It wasn't real*, I reminded myself. *How many women had he looked at like that?*

The carriage came to a stop, jolting me out of my memories. The night had been a dream. It was time to wake up. *A nightmare rather,*

I reminded myself. I had almost lost control. What if Siniy learned of the kiss?

A manservant opened the door and offered me a hand. Siniy himself stood before a bright, blue-painted manor hugged by bare trees. The only sign the estate had an end was the iron fence we had passed and city wall rising behind the house. You could not even see the neighboring manor. Never would I have expected anyone to own this kind of land inside the city.

"Welcome to your new home."

Siniy offered his arm, and I flashed back to how Alexei had done the same the previous evening. Blushing with shame at thinking of a man other than my soon-to-be husband, I took it. Thankfully, Siniy smiled at my heating cheeks, perhaps assuming they were the result of our proximity. It was, after all, the first time we touched.

His fine wool coat was softer than I had expected, his hand more elegant next to mine. Somehow, I had built up a monster in my mind and instead, a normal, handsome, if aging, man guided me forward. Both wives had died years ago—why would he have married them if he wished them dead? He could just have denied Popova or refused the wedding if he found me lacking.

"Does my home not please you?" Siniy asked, and I realized I had yet to greet him.

"It is more than I could ever have expected," I said, meaning every word. "Excuse me, Popova only said you would provide a home for me and the child. This is something else."

"Indeed. I have lived here all my life, and never plan to leave. It can get lonely, though."

Our boots crunched on the stone path, already clear of snow, as we approached the great door held open by a woman Siniy's age, her dress as black as any soldier's. As soon as we were through, she seemed to disappear.

A spiral staircase wide enough for a carriage dominated the entryway. Siniy stopped before it and pulled a clanging key chain from his suit pocket. Large and small, intricate and simple keys reflected the chandelier's light.

"I had them collect one of each key to each of the forty-nine doors of Blue Manor. This is my engagement gift—all the rooms are yours. My home belongs to you." He lifted the smallest key, the golden head shaped like a heart. "I only ask that you do not enter my study. That is my private space, such as every man needs. In there I conduct my research and document my discoveries. There are things which could hurt one such as yourself. To show my trust, I included even that."

My eyes locked on the keys as he flipped through them. "The whole manor is mine?"

"All of it. I only ask for the one room in the basement." He pressed the keys into my hand and my fingers instinctively closed. "Do you promise to stay out of it?"

I nodded, hardly listening, already imagining exploring.

"Good. Tonight is our engagement ball, the invites have already gone out, and tomorrow we sign the marriage contract. Dresses and finery wait in your chambers. I thought a masked ball was in order. Until then, I have work to do."

"That's... fast." Much faster than I had expected, as I had heard noble engagements often stretched on. "We hardly know each other."

His eyes drifted pointedly to my still flat midriff. "I thought you would be pleased, as time is of the essence."

Before I could find an answer, he left me with a dry kiss on my cheek. Shivers, the bad kind, raced down my back and fire swirled through my insides. The pressure was building, each day of insecurity and stress adding fuel. I only needed to get through the wedding and everything that night involved. Familiarity robbed fear of its power.

The woman who had opened the door appeared again and bowed.

"If the Lady pleases, I'll help you get ready."

Stunned to be addressed as *Lady*, I followed upstairs and, only when I was sure she could not see, wiped the kiss from my too-hot cheek while steadying my breathing, trying to slow the embers racing under my skin. *Could I use some of this wealth to learn how to use my magic safely? Could Siniy's research tell me how to control it?*

The gigantic house, old but well maintained, filled me with more apprehension than comfort—how could I, who only knew how to serve drunks, become the mistress of this place? My clenched fingers cramped around the many keys.

Nothing in the afternoon and early evening eased my worries. I was bathed and fed, my body and hair dressed, then left to discover my new home. While everyone else hurried to prepare for the party, I was the only one without a task. My free hand drifted to my midriff, reminding myself I had a purpose: to keep my child safe. So, unlocking all doors, I searched for anything amiss. What would clues of long dead wives even look like?

The keys turned smoothly, and each new room on the top floor, while seemingly long unused, had silk wall coverings, beds enough for dozens of guests, and polished furniture ready to be filled. The only occupied rooms were mine and what must be Lord Siniy's personal chambers. As he had not forbidden me from entering and seemed to be out of the house, I knocked, then tiptoed inside. A sitting room with well-used leather chairs and an organized desk greeted me. Through the next door stood his bedchamber. I avoided looking too long at the massive bed as I searched underneath, then through drawers and closets. Happy to escape it and the thoughts of how I would soon undress in here, I quickly moved into the bath chamber, then study. Letters seemed to race across the pages of books and notes. When I gave up on them, a headache pounded behind my eyes, and I decided most to be business correspondence I would barely understand even if I could read properly.

My heart plummeted.

The lord was disappointingly normal. At that thought, I realized I was searching for a reason to run. Something my practical side could accept. Because while Alexei's discoveries had seemed damning when alone on the barge, in this finely appointed manor filled with staff and light, I did not really believe whatever had happened to those women years ago would affect me.

I wanted a mystery where there probably was none. Sneaking about and inventing tales was not me. Deciding simply to ask Siniy when I saw him tonight, I returned to my chambers to rest. Tomorrow, I would marry and all would be well.

I raised the ornate golden basement key—the one place he had asked me to leave alone—and traced its head. The twisted lines, similar to sigils, shaped the open heart. It was strangely fine for a hidden away space, but he had talked about how important his research was—it was one of the few things I knew about the man. His fascination with magic the reason he wanted me and my child.

It made sense to not want my uneducated fingers to bumble about. What if I destroyed something priceless?

The unease rose again, and I quickly opened my heating hand, letting the keychain fall with a clank. Gold melted faster than most metals. I would not destroy what he had given me on the first day.

When I picked up the key, the upper part held a permanent impression of my thumb, as if proving why I should stay away from anything delicate. If my child did not inherit my powers, I would need to raise her from a distance. Afford wet-nurses and nannies. When I burned my sister, my mother called me a monster. If I hurt someone unintentionally again, she would be proven right. Pre-wedding jitters aside, surely with a house full of staff and the ability to hide away on this expansive land, I would never have to worry again. I would have all the help I could ever require.

The old woman who had showed me to my room, dressed me for the evening in a flowing red gown, rubies, and diamonds, and released my hair. In the full-length mirror, I saw myself as I never had before. There was nothing to straighten or fidget with. I had become one large flame. Disconcerting and empowering both. Grandpa would have hated it, for there was no hiding anymore. Despite all the taboos around magic and being a discreet man, Siniy seemed unafraid to make a statement, perhaps so no one would wonder why he married a common girl. One thing was sure: all eyes would be on me tonight.

The woman tied a mask covered in orange and yellow crystals around my face and smeared my lips with red tint, completing my transformation into a stranger. I imagined Alexei's amber eyes light up, seeing myself through his easy admiration, before I remembered how last night ended. Would Siniy pull me in for an equally claiming kiss? He had every right, while Alexei'd had none—but each man made my fire burn for all the wrong reasons. Tonight, I was a trophy to be paraded around, much like I had treated Alexei at the barge the night before, hoping old friends would notice and jump to conclusions. Maybe Siniy and I were not that different. Both lonely and wishing to impress our peers.

I shook out my hands, trying to rid myself of nerves and thoughts and memories, then focused on the image in the mirror. This was about me, not them. Ansa, with the straight skirt, starched jacket, and pinned hair had been replaced by a magical lady without fear. I was making my own opportunities instead of accepting what I got like Grandpa had.

The servant studied me with a frown instead of a smile. I should not be surprised not everyone in Siniy's household approved of the quick marriage, but something in her washed-out brown eyes raised the hairs on my neck. Alexei had guessed a jealous lover or murderous servant could have been behind the deaths. Could this woman, much closer to Siniy in age than I, be both?

With more of a nod than appropriate bow, she started to leave.

"What's your name?" I asked, trying to appear the lady and mistress of the house.

The woman sucked her lip, as if considering me, before answering. "Star Wind, if it pleases you."

Her voice said it had better. A pretty Sorchian name, but her accent was mostly Talian.

"Have you served Lord Siniy long?" How do you ask if someone killed his previous wives? If she's in love with her master? "Is he a good man?"

"Treat him with the respect he deserves. Every man needs his secrets. Be a good girl and look the other way."

Her eyes narrowed, lip twitching. Was she saying the lord took lovers? Had taken her, and I better stay out of it? I nodded quickly. I was already carrying an heir, perhaps I would not even need to see the inside of Siniy's bedchamber again.

Before Star Wind left, I gave her the borrowed dress and necklace, and requested it returned to the Midtown shop. She pursed her lips in judgment and question, then shook her head as if the mystery was not worth her energy or more time in my presence.

Relinquishing the dress severed the last connection to Alexei and our night. If I had kept it, I would have had a reason to seek him out. Or a physical memento that made it real. This was better. A clean break. He would surely go to the shop, and they would return the sigil ring. Or perhaps even send it to the palace. I paced back and forth, thoughts jumping like the Taliell in spring, Star Wind's words calming, then agitating as I turned them over.

When the knock on my door came, the sounds of laughter already drifted up from below, and I suddenly worried more about the judgment of strangers than my future husband's mysterious past.

Automatically checking my hair and dress, getting no peace from finding both free and flowing, I opened the door.

Siniy bowed to me in the doorway and offered his arm, his black coat detailed in burnt orange with buttons of amber and rubies. A matching pair.

We descended the spiral staircase as a sea of men and women dressed in the lush colors of night flowers and gems craned their necks in admiration. My body heated under their hungry gazes until I thought I would combust before we reached the bottom.

Siniy squeezed my hand, as if to remind me I was not alone, and led me through the crowd. I clung to him like a drunk to his tankard, hoping my poison would also cure all sorrows.

With the masks, they became interchangeable spectators glittering past, and I wondered as I met their eyes if they had been at the party last night. My own mask hid my blush, but they seemed to smirk at my fear. In my mind, the fine guests merged, their stares too similar behind hidden faces, until I indeed felt drunk despite not having touched a glass.

We arrived in a grand ballroom. I had walked its perimeter while the servants toiled to achieve the perfect polish, the sheen now hidden under uncaring feet. Somewhere, musicians played a slow tune, sounding more like a funeral than a wedding to my unrefined ears. As Siniy led me through dance steps I did not know, I became grateful for the slow pace. Perhaps that was why he had requested it.

"I rarely open my home, but a marriage deserves celebration. Two lives joined as one in eternity with complete trust," Siniy whispered in my ear as he pulled me close.

This was it. The time to calm my fears. Asking Star Wind had been the first step, talking to my future husband, the next. "I'm sorry to be insensitive, my lord, but... your previous wife. What happened to her?"

We spun again and his eyes seemed darker than before. "I actually had two, and it's not a pretty story. They were related—close as sisters. The first I courted only to discover she had a disease even the healers couldn't cure. She asked to marry on her deathbed. Her cousin became like family, and I proposed. She killed herself shortly after our wedding. I believe she couldn't bear to live her best friend's life. She wasn't ready to trust me and give me her heart."

"A tragedy," I said as the dance separated us again.

"It was years ago and has nothing to do with us. Don't let history taint our day."

You do not grow up poor without noticing when someone was trying to swindle you. Siniy sounded sincere, even grieving, but his careful eyes tracked me as if checking I believed his words. Maybe he just worried his new bride would mind two former wives. Maybe illness and suicide carried darker meanings. Maybe he suspected someone like Star Wind had been involved and chose to look the other way.

As the dance finished, I caught sight of a too-tall, too-familiar man watching us through a black mask. While Siniy dressed like a gentleman, Alexei seemed a highway robber, and, from how his eyes tracked me, I was the treasure he had come to take.

"Excuse me," I said to Siniy with a wobbly smile and real exhaustion. "I'm not used to so many people. Would you mind if I took a moment?"

He patted my hand. "You have been seen. Go to your room and rest."

But they had only seen my dress and mask and hair. I had expected him to ask me back, to want to introduce me to his guests, because even a recluse must have friends.

Confused, but determined not to question him on our first night, I slipped through the crowd. The black-clad highway robber matched my steps and despite what I had said last night about risking standing and marriage, I did not change my course or hurry my step.

"You must run," Alexei said, too loud. "Now."

I dared turn enough to look while my fiancé's eyes heated my back. "He has been nothing but courteous. For someone like me, this place is not something I can cast away," I whispered heatedly, barely moving my lips.

My anger from last night returned, knowing I was already not behaving like a *good girl,* much less a lady. Alexei could never understand what it meant to be poor. Worse. To be poor and a pregnant woman without family. Before coming here, the riches had been make-believe, now people moved out of my way with respect.

Alexei's large hand closed around my arm. "He'll kill you."

I stopped before the grand stairs. "He lost two wives to suicide and disease."

"There are at least seven dead women. *Please.*"

My eyes narrowed. "Prove it."

I could not throw this away on the word of a stranger. On rumors and tales. A man's false promises had brought me here. A man I had thought I knew. I thought loved me as I shared myself with him. Alexei bent over me, and the fear in his eyes was too real.

We stood there, frozen, alone in a garden of glittering people. He opened his mouth, and I thought he might offer me an alternative, ask me not to run but escape into the night *together*. Then he slammed it shut, and I remembered he was not the kind to marry.

Then Alexei was ripped away, and the world returned.

"You are bothering my wife."

Siniy placed a possessive hand on my back while two burly guards put theirs on Alexei's.

"She's not your wife yet," he spat, when a gorgeous man with tousled locks and tailored evening attire stepped up beside him and nodded to Siniy. He reminded me of an older, male version of the small healer who approached Alexei the night before.

"It seems my guest has been robbed of all senses at seeing your beautiful bride." The man turned to Alexei with a hard look. "We will be on our way."

"Prince Nikolai." Siniy bowed, paling though the stranger seemed friendly enough. "I'm honored you came."

Nikolai only nodded in return and waved the guards away, after a look from Siniy, they obeyed. When Alexei did not instantly walk toward the doors, Nikolai gave him a shove. And with a last long look, mouthing, *Don't marry him,* Alexei was gone.

"Make sure they leave and inform the gate guards that the tall one is not to be allowed inside again," Siniy said. He leaned closer to me until our breaths mixed, and I saw the threat in his eyes. "We all have a past. Make sure you leave it there. I am a private man and if someone steps uninvited onto my property, he'll not be seen again, no matter how high his friends are. You can have all this. Or nothing. Choose. In the morning, I'll be away to handle the last wedding arrangements and the servants will be given a day off to celebrate our marriage. Walk the house and consider what you're willing to lose."

Much as Nikolai had showed Alexei out, Siniy's hand steered me up the stairs as he followed a step behind. My back tensed under his touch as I wondered how much he had overheard. One of his feet dragged over the stones, as if an old injury slowed him.

At my door, I turned around to wish him good night, hoping to reassure him this would never happen again, only to find the hallway empty. Siniy must have stopped at the top of the stairs, though I could have sworn the footsteps followed. Knowing Alexei had gotten to me with his tales, despite he himself telling me not to trust rumors, I closed the door.

A moment later, the lock snapped shut.

Trapped, I listened to the distant sounds as the guests drank and danced the night away. In the softest bed I had ever known, I lay with Alexei's and Siniy's words spinning in my head, the keys turning in my hands. They represented everything this marriage offered, while Alexei brought nothing besides worries and a few laughs.

Still, when the sounds downstairs disappeared and dawn stained the air, the silence pressed in, and the Spirits of past brides hovered in my mind. *What if Alexei was right? Two wives could be explained away. Seven...*

The early sun pierced the light curtain, catching on something lying on the dresser. First, I thought it just another piece of jewelry—it seemed I would have a great many—then I recognized the heavy ring with the tree inside the sigil border. Alexei's ring. Star Wind must have received it in exchange for the dress and necklace.

I closed my fingers around it, finding it heavier than expected. Did it symbolize the familial expectations he tried to escape? If I had it last night, I could have returned it. The solidity centered me. I wanted to be a tree with deep roots, allowing me to reach the sky. Perhaps that was why I could not resist slipping it on. Despite being too large—made for a man's hands—it felt righter than any of the precious stones Siniy had hung on me.

Behind me, the lock clicked. I spun and jerked the door open. The hallway stood as empty as last night.

I crept down the stairs still in my fine gown—without help, I could not open the buttoned back. But I needed not have bothered sneaking.

The manor was empty.

As Siniy had said, I was alone.

CHAPTER NINE

ALEXEI

I would have earned another beating—two in a three-day, a lot even for me—had Nikolai not been present. He was a dichotomy—a man with little official power, who desired none, but still the second in line to the throne. If he wore something, it became the latest fashion, if he attended an event, it became the place to be. How many would have shown up tonight had I not convinced him to accept Siniy's invite?

Guards who probably had little understanding of who Nikolai was bowed deeply, sensing that someone who took themselves so seriously must be too high for them to challenge. He could probably get away with murder just due to his bearing. If Dimi did not return, this man would be king. As he fixed his already perfect hair, I shivered at the thought.

"Well, that was that," Nikolai said when we were alone.

"*That?* I have to go back. She didn't listen."

He shrugged. "You delivered your message. What else is there to do?"

"He'll *kill her.*"

Nikolai spread his hands. "To honor my cousin, I got you into the party, but I'm no fighter, ready to challenge guards and a house full of guests only to drag away an unwilling woman."

His words stopped me. Tales, rumors and second-hand information would not do. Ansa had asked for proof, and for that—

"I need to get back inside."

"So you said. How? Break down the door?" Nikolai laughed.

I scowled at the man who had never taken a risk beyond a daring outfit. "If I need to."

Nikolai shook his head at me but did not ask for details before heading in the direction of his waiting carriage. He had been seen with me tonight. Presumably he wanted to be able to honestly deny any involvement from here on out.

Accompanied only by the occasional Spirit, I stayed in the darkness blanketing this far corner of North's Place. Anyone who could afford to live here was wealthy, and the size of Siniy's estate spoke of unimaginable funds. That, together with his obscurity, whispered of secrets and of a man who could afford to kill his brides to protect them.

Soon, the guests trailed out, presumably on their way to the next party as the prince had already left and the mysterious bride been seen. Undoubtedly, I had fed the rumor mill enough tonight that they would still be talking by summer. They would say Siniy stole Ansa from me, or perhaps she had been involved with the crown prince, her rejection the reason he left Tal. Or she was Nikolai's last lover—or even his current one. From here, the tales would only grow. I had caused all the damage Ansa had feared when I kissed her. Something inside me squirmed at the fraction of a chance that I was wrong, and I had irrevocably harmed her reputation the night before she entered the nobility.

I shook my head. That risk was nothing against death. Better she place a mage's curse—magic which could not be fought or controlled—on me afterward.

The snow fell heavily on my shoulders and the perfect manors hiding corruptions and excesses. Shivers shook me as I brushed off my finest coat, having left my outdoor gear in Nikolai's coach. Letting the memory of Ansa's fire warm me, I leaned onto a tree wishing the bare branches provided more cover.

When finally the last carriage trailed away, and I was about to leave my hidden post, a line of servants exited, as if the lord was readying for travel, leaving the mansion empty.

Siniy's blue coach pulled up to the lanterns as he stopped to speak with the guards. Then he too left. Only Ansa and the men at the gate seemed to remain. Something would happen tonight.

Three Spirits drifted closer, illuminating the empty street, and heralding death to come. This time, my shivers had nothing to do with the cold.

Rather than iron plate and sword, the guards patrolled the gate in leathers and fur with bludgeoners strapped to their belts. They stayed inside the lantern light, squinting into the darkness. Had there only been two, I would have pushed my bad luck further. With four, I could admit defeat without throwing a single punch. Instead, I tried to scale the well-kept walls. The second time I fell on my ass and had to scurry away as they investigated the sound, I despaired. At least they did not follow my steps in the fresh snow.

My options dwindled before me.

I could not bribe the guards, for Siniy possessed infinitely more wealth.

I could not ask von Uster for help, for he had made clear he would stay out of it until there was concrete evidence.

I no longer had Dimi, who besides offering advice, could have commanded the City Guard without question.

Nikolai had made his position clear.

Dawn lightened the air. The snowfall abated. Today they would marry. If Ansa lived that long. When would Lord Siniy return? I needed to get inside. Needed someone who could beat down the guards and the door like I had told Nikolai.

A mad plan formed in my mind. If it worked, von Uster would back me. If not, only with the Wishmaker's blessing would I live to escape to my family estate to lick my wounds.

As the winter sun chased the Spirits away, I ran down the empty streets, slipping in the sludge. Ansa's boss owed me a beatdown, and with a few half-truths of my own, I planned to collect.

I moved from the richest to the poorest quarters of Tal as the sun steadily climbed and the street cleaners came out to brush away the snow. There were no coaches to hire this early, no vendors barring my way. Not familiar enough with Midtown and Rivertown to cut through alleys, I stayed on the main roads and focused only on running while silently praying I would not be too late.

My tired mind barely registered crossing the bridge where Ansa and I first talked. It seemed I only blinked before I stood in front of the run-down drink hall and pounded on the door. Sweat stuck the shirt to my back, the cold of the night forgotten. After wiping my face, I threw away the cravat Nikolai had insisted on and beat the door until finally someone cursed on the upper floor.

A window shutter slammed open, and the bleary-eyed proprietor stuck his head out.

"We're closed. Go away!"

"Now you're open." I stepped back so he could see me and raised my hand dramatically, imitating a fire bearer in a play I once saw in Rivertown. "Or you never open again."

He blinked at me, then my hand, and the blood left his face. The head disappeared, the door clicked open, and a bowing, cowering version of the man showed me inside.

I tried to stand like Dimi or Nikolai would, like my word could bring another to their knees. In reality, my punch would certainly have more effect, and by now, I longed to hit something.

"I knew you would come," the owner said before I could get a word out. "A man such as you must have a purpose to visit Low-town. I know things."

I nodded gravely to hide my confusion, while internally time ticked away. Would Siniy already have returned? Another thought struck me: was Ansa even alive in there? Maybe the lord and his staff had left for a country estate, her corpse packed into a suitcase or burned to ash, denying even her Spirit peace. As a fire bearer, she should have been able to defend herself, but if he had come upon her unexpectedly or drugged her...

"Many underhanded deals go down here. Last night, the—"

I raised my hand again and the man, who had continued speaking while I panicked, froze like I had pressed a blade to his throat. "I'll return to hear it all. First, I have a debt to settle. Where do I find the men who attacked me?"

"Who?"

I rarely got angry. Most things rolled off me, for I would much rather laugh than shout, but now, I let all the frustration from the last week's events show. "Should I settle my debt with you instead?"

The man backed away, waving me toward the door. "Two streets to the left, then one over. The pink house. They and their friends rent it together."

"The Roja thanks you," I said, channeling the spymaster's threatening smile.

The barkeep paled further at the casual mentioning of the secret police. Hopefully, von Uster would not mind. I needed all the clout I could get.

Outside, I only paused to discard the coat and roll up my sleeve, exposing the swirling noble's sigil I usually kept hidden. Despite only being a fifth the size of Dimi's, it seemed too large, a brand I had not consented to. Something I could never escape. But today, all it implied would help. With the winter sun at my back, I set off down the street, not quite running but letting my long legs eat the ground. It was time to make a spectacle of myself. To execute a prank beyond anything Dimi and I ever did, and if it went wrong, there was no one else to take the blame. It was time to do something that mattered.

The pink house was indeed where the barkeep had said, and eight men, each larger and more muscled than the last, dressed in worn rough-spun work shirts, without coats despite the cold, exited. There was little work for orchard workers before spring, but the call for day laborers would start soon. Most of them would be shoveling snow and breaking ice until the weather turned.

I placed myself in the middle of the street, like a tree trying to halt boulders, and raised my sigiled hand, naked without the ring, in the universal sign to stop. The leading two came to an abrupt halt, almost tripping those behind.

I forced a dangerous smile to cover my ragged breaths and turned my mad dash into a saunter while pointing at them. "You owe me, and your friends can help to pay, or you'll all be without a home. Perhaps all of Lowtown will burn for your offence."

I twisted my hand with flair, though Ansa had done nothing similar to call the flames. Thankfully, showmanship was its own magic.

"We meant to return your money," the closest, baldest one stammered. Stalking forward, I realized his lack of hair was not natural for he lacked even eyebrows. It had been burnt away.

"It's too late for that." I lifted both arms, as if ready to throw my terrible power at them, and all eight cowered.

"We'll do anything, please," the hairless leader exclaimed as the others nodded.

"Excellent." I twisted on the spot and waved for them to follow. "Bring your axes. I have a door for you to break down."

Retrieving my last funds from my boot, I paid for two coaches to take us back across Tal. When we arrived, Siniy's blue coach was back in the driveway behind the gate. Again, I was too late.

Panic clawed inside as I pointed at the manor.

"Get me inside and I'll forget I ever saw you. Don't let anyone stand in your way."

The bald one, who had said to call him Keep and named himself the leader, looked from me to the sprawling, well-to-do estate, as if trying to judge the bigger monster.

"The Roja commands it," I said as I marched on the staring gate guards. They had been hired to handle drunk guests and the occasional thief. At a frontal assault such as Tal had not seen in recent memory, one hid in the gatehouse while the others advanced, loosening their bludgeoners as if preparing for a brawl.

I had failed to stand up for Dimi, frozen instead of risking my own skin. It did not matter that my actions would not have changed the outcome. I had owed him to try. I would not do the same with Ansa. She would not be another dust-gathering death certificate. Von Uster could decide whether to hang me or not for my actions tomorrow.

With a shout echoing through the impeccable North's End, I rushed forward.

Behind me, the giants followed.

CHAPTER TEN

ANSA

When the servants hurried to clean and prepare, the manor had seemed busy, foreign and fascinating. When finely dressed guests filled the many rooms, it had been bustling and desirable. Walking the halls alone, I found the vastness eerie and abandoned. Every time I rounded a corner, I expected someone to greet me and explain that the others would be along any moment; instead, only the clinking of the keys accompanied my steps.

When Siniy had said he was giving the servants a day off in celebration of our union, I had not expected them all to leave—was this how nobles ran their households?

I tiptoed through each room, trying not to disturb the oppressive silence. The hairs on my neck stood up while my skin stretched too tight over restless embers, as it felt like eyes followed me. As if the house itself watched.

Again and again, I stopped to breathe through my nerves and smother the fire that threatened to erupt and defend me from an invisible threat. My hair was too loose, hiding my peripheral vision, the dress tangling in my legs every time I spun to look behind. Briefly, I considered finding a knife and cutting myself out of it. Only the careful stitches, weeks of someone's labor, stopped me. Despite the fire in my veins, I desired to create, not destroy.

The ballroom stood empty, velvet curtains drawn. Scuffs on the wooden floor, the only sign of last night's celebration. I drifted along the walls, unable to bring myself to step into the empty space, as hidden eyes seemed to travel up my body, my pounding heart making sparks dance around my fingers.

I clenched my hands and eyes shut, suffocating feelings and fire, until only emptiness remained. As a child, at Grandpa's instruction, I had meditated for bells, until I held only cold clarity. Somehow, in the whirlwind of emotions since fall, I had forgotten how.

Siniy had spoken true—I needed to decide who to believe, what life to live. Alexei had offered no proof, and I knew how quickly a tale of two dead wives could have grown to seven. Perhaps there had been a failed engagement in-between and everyone spoke of murder. If I did not find answers today, I would sign the marriage contract. There were no assurances in life. We could only make the best possible choices with the information available at the time. I refused to leave and always wonder *what if*.

In the morning sun, I walked the grounds, finding only empty flowerbeds and bare rose stalks bent under their white blanket. Summer would bring colors. Here, my child could learn to walk. Play without fear of torching all of Tal. I could see it so clearly, hear the laughter.

Inside again, I moved with purpose despite leaving wet spots of melted snow behind. This was going to be my home. I was no haunting Spirit. I was no longer hiding. Striding through the halls, I used the keys to unlock all rooms. After the thirty-eighth—a kitchen cupboard—I had found nothing more suspicious than a closet full of fine dresses. My stomach twisted at the thought of a former Lady Siniy wearing them, possibly even the one I had on, but it told me nothing more than that the lord was a miser despite his great wealth. It was not the first time I wore hand-me-downs, but after marrying, I swore it would be my last.

And then I realized I had made my decision. Tonight, I would become a noble. My child would be born and raised here. He or she would never experience my hardships.

The decision should have calmed the fire. Instead, it swirled in my center, a blaze growing hotter and hotter the longer I ignored the last key. Back in the entry hall, I faced the door blocking the downward turn of the stairs.

Siniy had only asked one thing of me. It should have been an easy request. Be a *good girl* Star Wind had said. But the fire burned and burned, threatening to escape despite my decision. I needed to quiet it. I needed to see what my future husband hid or I might soon wake in a smoldering ruin. I would not touch anything, break anything. What could a peek hurt?

The basement door did not have a lock. It swung open under my questioning hand, revealing the narrow staircase, darkness and hidden secrets. Somewhere below me was the final locked room.

Damning Alexei for messing with my head, telling myself I was being silly, praying to the Wishmaker to find nothing, I strode down the steps. Too soon, the light from above disappeared. I slowed, clutching the sigil ring still on my finger.

Had I been trained better, I could have summoned a mage light, as the nobles were said to do. I considered trying but the fire in my blood had grown too great—if I let out a spark, a storm might follow.

I rushed back up to search the house, finally finding a candle in the kitchen cupboard but turned over a sack of flour in my hurry. The white cloud stuck to my fine dress and covered the floor, but something inside me screamed time was running out. I would clean later. After brushing off as best I could, I lit the candle in the still smoldering hearth, then, with a steadying breath, descended back into the dark.

The chill of the stones seeped through my fine slippers. The only sounds accompanying me were the swish of my skirts and the clink of the keys. I rubbed the rough swirls of my fingerprint on the heart shaped one.

The further I went, the more sensible arguments arose. I should turn away, clean the kitchen. If I could not trust my husband enough to keep one room to himself, I should not marry him. Still, I walked with measured steps ever down. The flour probably clung to my slippers, proving I already disregarded his words.

The houses in Lowtown and Rivertown rarely had basements as the Taliell flooded most springs, and even in North's Place, I had expected to walk down only a few steps but long after the light above had disappeared, my candlelight had yet to reach the bottom.

I moved silently despite feeling alone in the world, trapped by the earth on both sides. A scrape came from above, like the door slowly closing. Then again. Closer.

Scratch. Scratch. Scratch.

Fear boiled my blood. My palms burned.

It's only rats, I told myself and hurried on.

The unfamiliar skirt twisted around my legs. I stumbled against the wall and melting wax dripped between my fingers. The softened candle stump slipped from my hand and extinguished.

I clenched the keys, scrambling to remain upright. My knee slammed into flat floor, shooting pain up and down my leg. In the pitch black, I had reached the end of the stairs.

Instead of gravel or rough-cut stone, my hands and knees rested on smooth, icy squares laid in regular patterns. Mosaics perhaps. I crawled forward, though I wanted nothing more than to go back. Maybe if I asked Siniy before signing the marriage contract, he would take me here himself. I knew nothing of magic research. There could be a perfectly reasonable explanation for keeping it so far under the main house. I would find a way to tame the magic without answers. I should have listened to Grandpa and accepted the world as is.

My hand touched something wet and cold, smearing the ring still on my finger and sticking to my hand. Fighting to not retract in horror, I felt a freezing metal door before me. Scrambling from one wall to the other, finding them both solid, I knew I was trapped. I had reached the end of the tunnel.

The scraping was closer. Louder.

Wetness soaked into my clothes, but I barely noticed. Rats had not seemed so bad when there still was light. Now they grew in my mind, and I stumbled to my feet. My left knee screamed in pain as I put weight on it. Leaning on the metal wall, I felt a keyhole under my sticky hand. I flinched as if bitten when an iron-tinged scent reached my nose.

Terror at what might wait behind the door and what approached on the stairs overwhelmed me. Involuntary flames erupted, the flash revealing a golden door and the partly dried crimson flowing out under it. It matched my red dress and hair, and the jewels and mask

I had been given—assuming Siniy thought of fire when he looked at me, not blood.

The wick of the broken candle caught fire before the flames went out. The scraping came again, like steps on stairs. With shaking fingers, I retrieved the candle, then, because I had come too far, because the evidence already stained my skin, I slid the heart-headed, blood-stained key into the lock.

It must be from animals.

Disgust filled me at the thoughts of what Siniy might use them for.

If it's bad, I'll run.

The key turned with a click.

I need proof.

The door opened.

Twisting glass beakers, tubes and liquids reflected my light—like a mad version of Popova's ordered apothecary shopwindow. Sconces with thick candles lined the closest wall. Conquering my fear, I lit them, revealing a square room with two sides covered in books. The trail of blood ended at the final wall where five levels of wide shelves carried seven shapes covered by golden cloths.

Part of me knew what I would find before I pulled the first one off.

Despite the sunken features of the dead, naked woman, she seemed to stare back at me.

Her blond hair was still perfect, her eyes wide in fear. The red cut bisecting her bloodless neck, and below, where her heart should have been, a gaping red hole met my eyes.

I ripped away cloth after cloth. The next body was the same, and the one after that. On each shelf, two women rested. Except the last, which held an empty space. There lay a folded cloth and surgical knives—my place.

The scraping sounded directly behind me. A shape much too large for a rat blocked the candlelight. I recoiled and was caught in a tight embrace.

Fire swirled at the tip of my fingers as the knife dug into my neck.

"You burn me, and you won't remain alive long enough to bear the child." Siniy's voice, more animated than ever before, breathed heavily into my ear. "I could have killed you before you knew what happened, should have for how you betrayed me, but the child makes you an exception."

I was back under the water, struggling for breath, but this time I was not fighting for myself. "You'll never have her."

"I swore it would be my heir, and so far, only one of us has broken their promises. All I asked for was a wife who'll stay true. You even wear another's ring. How can I trust anything you say?"

"Why?" I whispered, my eyes locked on the gaping holes in the women's chests.

His breath heated my neck, and it took all my willpower to not press further into the sharp blade to get away.

"You mages are ignorant of your true power, wasting it all," Siniy said. "And when I share my life, offer you everything, you break my trust. Show your worthlessness." He caressed my neck with the knife blade. "But I'll still make something out of you. And one day a woman of magic and beauty will be my wife. Until then, I'll be content with your parts."

"The hearts?"

He smacked his lips. "Delicious, though ineffective." His hand traced my chest, then stomach. "Maybe I was wrong. Maybe it's in the liver. The elixir will work and power will belong to those who earned it."

Far above, wood splintered with a crash and footsteps, so different from the slow scratching, pounded down the stairs.

"Ansa!"

Siniy swung us around so that I stood between him and the door. The knife pressed harder, and a hand slammed over my mouth before I could answer. In moments, Alexei'd descended the stairs I had painstakingly crawled down. He stopped in the doorway with murder in his normally twinkling eyes.

"Get away, or she's dead," Siniy said, just as calmly as he had everything else. "Your prince is already gone, and if you don't leave, I'll use all my power to ensure you do not survive the night. Don't throw your life away for the likes of her."

"There are no *likes of her*." Alexei's eyes never left mine. "No one burns as bright."

Siniy snorted. "They're all the same on the inside, only the outside dazzles. Magic is dying in the nobility. People like us who should have it are born without, while the likes of her waste it."

"There's no waste. *Trust me,* I'm not leaving." Alexei's eyes implored me. "Only her will keeps her from burning down the world. She can save herself, just needs a little help from someone who doesn't mind getting singed."

His eyes flickered to the knife as he surreptitiously lifted his hand.

Like the night we met, he needed me to burn. Then, he had taken the beating for me. Would he take on the knife this time?

Fear froze me, while inside, flames consumed. If I let them out, they could take us all. My entire life, I had been terrified of the destruction I could cause. Once the fire was free, it was its own creature, eating and growing. Would the air in this room even be enough?

Maybe Alexei saw the terror in my eyes. Maybe it was the surety that the longer this standoff lasted, the lower a chance we had of walking away. Maybe he saw something in Siniy's face or a twitch in his hand.

As the knife cut deeper and a drop of blood trailed down my neck, Alexei leaped. Last time I saw him fight, he was half drunk. This time, his hands wrapped around Siniy's forearm and halted the knife before I knew what happened.

Responding to the shock, the fire exploded. And I let it. The pleasure of letting go, of being an uninhibited creature of flame, unstoppable like the Goddess herself, swept through me.

Blue and red, yellow and orange blazed. Behind me, Siniy screamed, and inside, I heard my sister when I hurt her as a child. Heard my mother's curses. I burned hotter, wishing for the fire to consume the memories. Begging it to take everything away.

The flames filled the room until only the amber eyes locked on mine remained. Part of me recognized them, the rest sought to escape it all.

"It's over," a familiar voice I no longer knew said, barely audible over the roaring in my head.

The desire to incinerate the world grew.

"I trust you," the voice said, and something inside responded. "Ansa, stay with me."

Ansa. That was the name of a girl even her grandfather, who cared for her and trained her, had not trusted. Who had been promised love again and again only to discover another lie. A girl who always suppressed her anger, though inside she burned with it.

Rough hands held my scorching arms. Belief shone in his watering eyes.

With an inhale, the flames retreated under my skin.

"There you are." A smile twisted his lips before he sank to the floor in a coughing fit.

The magic still sang through me. I was alive and powerful. Free and strong. I knew the aftereffects loosened my control, but what I desired was not destruction. For once, there was no need to fight.

Sinking down beside him, I pressed my still hot lips to his. Magic use might remove inhibitions, and we might not have a future, but he trusted me, and in this moment, that was exactly what I needed. There would be enough time to deal with the world. Perhaps he had used me. Perhaps I was using him. I no longer cared.

His arms pulled me close, and a different kind of heat entered the kiss as our tongues met, and again, I let myself go.

The truth burned inside—I did not need anyone to save me, only to accept me as I was. No tests or lies. He did not need to promise me anything, because when it really mattered, he had come.

CHAPTER ELEVEN

ALEXEI

My room had become infinitely more inviting, though the only thing added was Ansa. A calmness spread inside me, something soft and fragile and new, as I watched her sleep off the effect of using too much magic. She wore one of my shirts, overly long on her, and my sigil ring, deformed but still recognizable, on her finger. I ignored the grand watch and its swinging pendulum. The sun seemed to be setting outside, but day and night had meant little the last few days.

After we exited the basement, she had looked truly adrift, with no place to call home, so I brought her here. We had fallen into a dead sleep after washing the worst of the soot off and discarding the ruined clothing. Her soft snores turned the lonely room homey.

Unable to sleep, my eyes landed on the papers I had taken from Siniy's manor after finding Ansa, then traveled to the unanswered letter from my father. Finally, I knew just what to write.

Night came, and with ink-splotched fingers, I pulled Ansa close, watching her until I could no longer keep my eyes open. With a sigh, I rested my head on the shared pillow. There was still time for sleep. And maybe something more.

A soft knock cracked our cocoon. Before sleep fully left me, I stood between Ansa and the door, knife drawn. I had known my actions last night would have consequences, but I had not thought they would arrive so soon.

Another knock, harder this time.

"I know you're in there. Both of you. Open up."

Von Uster's normally clipped voice sounded almost jolly. I placed the knife on the bed, within Ansa's reach. Arresting me might be just the kind of thing to bring the man joy. If there were guards on the other side, it was pointless for me to resist. She was another matter. For her, I would fight one last time. Hopefully, they would lock me up somewhere Dimi could get me when he returned. Ansa could have chosen a life of ignorance, but despite the consequences, she had chosen knowledge. I would not run from my actions again.

I unlocked and flicked open the door. Von Uster strode in, owning the space around him. No one followed. That did not mean I could relax. Having the spymaster in my chambers while half-dressed seemed more wrong than being placed in chains.

"So this is the special friend you went to so much trouble for." He waved toward Ansa as she pulled the blanket up to her neck, awakened by his knocks. "Don't worry, my dear, you're not my type." He turned to me. "It has been a most invigorating night. I have been expecting your report for hours."

Belatedly, I remembered to bow. "I'm sorry, my lord. I was coming to tell you—"

"That you've been busy using my name and burning nobles."

"It wasn't Alexei's fault, it was mine. Siniy would have killed me," Ansa said unusually quietly, and I wished she had not. She did not know it, but there were enough strikes against my name. There was no need to tarnish hers. Especially with a babe on the way.

Von Uster gave me a considering look before sighing. "Despite the fire, we found enough to sentence the lord thrice over. The King has decreed Siniy's estate claimed by the crown. A nice piece of property that, so everything worked out for the best."

"That was your intention?" I could not keep the incredulity from my voice. I had been so glad von Uster shared information and his support, however limited, that I had not questioned further the most secretive man in Tal giving something away for free.

The spymaster grinned. "It wouldn't have looked good if someone acted on the king's orders and then he took the land—especially land he already has plans for. That's just the kind of thing that raises the nobles' ire. A bride and her supposed lover revealing a dark truth though. No one will speak up on Siniy's behalf now."

"We're done then?" I could not keep the anger from my voice. I had been used. Expertly.

"There are a few pieces I would love for you to clarify. Who did you recruit to break down the doors? The tales of you leading the charge are quite dramatic."

"Giants," I said curtly. "Who owed me a favor."

"Does that have anything to do with your previous bear wrestling?"

"Bears in Tal?" Ansa interjected, and I could not keep my lips from twitching. For once, a rumor I could fully support.

"And what are your future plans?" von Uster asked, seeming to address both of us.

"I..." Ansa's voice shook as if the full reality of her situation caught up with her.

"My father owns apple orchards outside Denyev. There would be a place for you," I said before she had to complete the sentence. "My sister would love you."

"And you?" she asked, completely ignoring the spymaster watching our exchange.

"I belong here." *I owed it to Dimi to be here when he returned.* The king couldn't mean to keep him away long. Then... It might be time to visit home again.

Ansa turned away, though not before I saw the disappointment in her eyes as she placed my sigil ring on the nightstand.

I wet my lips, seeking the words to explain, when von Uster clapped his hands together. "A Lowtown barkeep is waiting. No time to dally."

"For me?" My confusion must have been written across my face.

"You claimed to be a Roja, and your investigative skills, while lacking in refinement, were adequate. The King was very pleased by your part in bringing Siniy's assets to the crown. And you want him very pleased, if you are to be in any position to help your prince when he is allowed back to Tal."

Von Uster threw a medallion at me. By reflex, I snatched it out of the air only to find the dreaded three crossed bones of the Roja facing me. Taking that as acceptance—for what other answer was there?—von Uster sauntered out, whistling. I almost missed the frowning face he usually showed the world.

"I can really live with your family?" Ansa asked, seemingly ignorant that the course of my life had just changed. I guess hers had as well. "What will they think?"

"That the babe is mine." I picked up two letters from my desk and offered them to her. "If you want it to be."

She blinked back at me. "Yours?"

"My mother would be delighted. It's only through the Wishmaker's blessing, it has not happened already." I pushed the letters I had prepared into her unresponsive hands. "Why not wish again and make it so? In another world, we met months ago. Spent the summer on river barges and enjoyed each other's company. My mother knows I cannot support a child here, not now with Dimi gone, so I asked you to go Sizov. No one would question it."

"In this world, we fell in love?"

She smiled and the now-familiar embers glowed in her blue eyes. I sank down on the bed next to her, the softness inside my chest expanding.

"Very much so. I already wrote we'll be heartbroken to be apart. Luckily, I sometimes visit." Her hand closed around mine, unnaturally warm, worn from work, and absolutely perfect. "The country is calm. My family is far from Lord Siniy's wealth, but you and your child will be well taken care of. I think you might like it there."

I bent to kiss her softly, this time for no other reason than that I wanted to.

Her lips caressed mine before she rested her head on my chest and whispered, "I trust you."

Chapter Twelve

Ansa

The carriage rocked as it left Tal on the winter-hardened Pilgrim's Road. The incessant steppe wind cleared it of snow, howling despite the closed windows. In summer, those seeking a moment more with their dead's Spirits flocked to Tal. Sellers hawked wares and innkeepers room and board. The cold months left it empty and frozen. For the next three weeks, this carriage would be my home. I wished again I could have persuaded Alexei to join me. Before leaving, I had worried about what reception I would receive from his family when arriving alone. Now, I imagined the pleasure this journey could have been with his company. But the cheerful old man who had invaded his room last night would not allow it, and Alexei had convinced me he was not to be ignored.

At least a letter was flying with griffon to warn his family of my arrival. No matter how much Alexei had assured me I would be welcome, worry swirled through my veins. The magic felt different since I had let it out, no longer about to boil over. When I did not clutch it as tightly, it became easier to control. Even wearing Alexei's too-large, creased clothes I did not fidget. Appearances did not matter like they had because I was not trying to hide the monster inside behind starched skirts. In Siniy's underground study, I had seen what real monsters did. How fine clothes and money only made them worse. No matter what my mother had said, that was not me. I could also not be invisible like Grandpa had wished. Instead, I intended to use what had been given to me to be good. Let others judge me by that instead of my appearance.

As the city wall disappeared in a white flurry, I pulled out the heavy letter Alexei had given me with instructions not to open it until I was too far gone to turn around. Despite what had happened with Siniy, I followed the directions. When I had said I trusted Alexei, it had been the truth.

I broke the sigil-stamped wax and unfolded an official-looking document. The skulls and roses of Tal decorated the corners, swirling letters emblazoned in gold declared it official and binding, blessed by King and Goddess.

Though I had never seen one before, I recognized it for what it was. A noble marriage contract.

With a shaking finger, I traced the names—mine, then *Rostya Ti Zakharov of House Siniy* crossed out and scribbled next to it in black ink *Alexei Semyon Yurievich of House Denyev*. When I lifted the paper closer to the window, sure the light was playing a trick on my mind, a note fell out.

Ansa—Burn the contract or be the lady. It fits you better anyway.

My eye caught gold glinting on the carriage floor. I must have dropped it when I unfolded the larger documents. I picked up the ring. More oblong now than round. Damaged but still wearable. The tree remained, its branches stretching to the sky.

Tears stained my cheeks as I slipped it on. They evaporated before they fell, turning the air foggy. One man had tried to own and destroy me. The other had let me go and given me the means to grow my own roots.

I wanted to order the driver to turn around. But instead, I let her take me and my child to our new life, knowing this was not the end, but a beginning. Spring would come, Alexei would visit, and I would thank him in person. Surely, I would be able to show him that together, the countryside could be far from boring.

Inside me, something fluttered for the first time, as if to confirm there was more than one kind of adventure worth having.

If you enjoyed Unlocking Fire, please let others know on Amazon and Goodreads. Your reviews are what makes books a success!

Ansa and Alexei's story finishes in Spinning Fire in October 2024!

Pre-order now and get it for ~~$4.99~~ $2.99

Need something to tie you over? Read on for a free Alexei short story.

Wondering what happens when Dimitri returns to Tal?

Read the competed Cinderella retelling duology, Stealing Glass & Claiming Glass, NOW!

FREE ALEXEI AND ANSA SHORT STORY

Read what happens when Alexei meets Ansa again in *Returning Home* by scanning the QR code below

Returning Home
An Ansa and Alexei short story

Want to know what happens when Dimitri returns to Tal?
The story continues on **Stealing Glass: A Cinderella Retelling**

THE TALE OF BLUEBEARD

Every fairy tale has a moral and most are universal enough to be applied today, centuries after the tales' origin. That is probably why they stay with us and get told again and again. As they came from oral storytelling, there are many regional variations of each—making modern fairy tale retellings part of a long tradition.

Bluebeard is one of the few in which, in any original versions I have come across, magic occurs. It has no curses, witches, fairy godmothers, or talking animals, besides the human kind. While Tal is a world of magic, where the dead reside among the living, I wanted to keep the "big bad" and people's motivations human. The main thing I changed, from my view, is that while the original bride was saved by her brother, Ansa can save herself.

I also tweaked the moral.

Several interpretations of the original stories claim the lesson people were meant to take away from it was to listen to your husband. I cannot believe this is what any modern reader would take away. Perhaps instead, know the person you are about to marry, or if it seems too good, there is usually a hidden cost.

In *Unlocking Fire*, I wanted to make it about trust in all its forms—earned, broken, expected, and lost. In the end, each reader decides what the book was about, so only you can tell me if I was successful.

If you have a minute to spare and want to listen to or read one of the many publicly available versions of Bluebeard, this is the one I took the epigraph from: https://etc.usf.edu/lit2go/68/fairy-tales-and-other-traditional-stories/4858/blue-beard/

WHO IS LIV STROM?

Liv is a Swedish author raising her three children on fairy tales.

For the last ten years, she has lived in Zurich, Switzerland, and enjoy exploring the lakes, mountains and medieval towns. Her main writing companion is her wild beagle, Amazing Louis of the Whispering Hunters (he came with the name and a long and proud pedigree). As a writer with aphantasia—she cannot visualize anything in her mind—she considers it a magic power to make her characters live in yours.

Her stories usually feature kick-ass women and have appeared in *Apex, Hexagon SF Magazine,* and *Mystery Magazine,* among others, and been included on Tor.com's Must-Read Speculative Fiction and reviewed on Locus.

You can find all Liv's stories on http://www.livstromwriters.comand rare posts (which hopefully will be more frequent when she overcomes her innate introversion) on @AuthorLivStrom(Instagram) and @LivStromWrites(TikTok).

Acknowledgements

Thank you to my family who allowed me to hide in the attic to write this, especially my youngest as it was drafted in during her naps.

A book is never written in isolation. This one might not have been written at all without a very special beta reader who said "No body, no death" and made me believe Alexei's story deserved more. So if you enjoyed the story, thank Ally.

9 783907 446201